BACK ON THE BLOCK

Also by Felicia Madlock

Sins of the Father

BACK ON THE BLOCK

Felicia Madlock

www.urbanbooks.net

Urban Books
1199 Straight Path
West Babylon, NY 11704

ISBN-13: 978-1-60162-054-5
ISBN-10: 1-60162-054-3

First Trade Paperback Printing: January 2007
First Mass Market Paperback Printing: August 2008
Printed in the United States of America

10 9 8 7 6 5 4 3 2 1

*This is a work of fiction. Any references or similarities to actual
events, real people, living, or dead, or to real locales are in-
tended to give the novel a sense of reality. Any similarity in
other names, characters, places, and incidents is entirely coinci-
dental.*

Distributed by Kensington Publishing Corp.
Submit Wholesale Orders to:
Kensington Publishing Corp.
C/O Penguin Group (USA) Inc.
Attention: Order Processing
405 Murray Hill Parkway
East Rutherford, NJ 07073-2316
Phone: 1-800-526-0275
Fax: 1-800-227-9604

Prologue

"Get your ass from under that chair, girl, or I'm gonna—" Tracey's mother stopped mid-sentence as she watched her daughter dart from under the chair to the opposite side of the room.

In her desperate effort to get out of her mother's reach, Tracey fell onto the coffee table. An unfinished glass of Hennessy, a can of Coke, and a plate of half-eaten chicken toppled to the floor. Her eyes bulged in horror as she turned to see her mother's raised arm cut swiftly through the air. She felt the hot, immediate sting of the leather belt slice her upper arm. Her thin, high-pitched, six-year-old shrieks filtered outside, breaking the rhythm of the neighborhood kids singing their rhymes and jumping Double Dutch on the sidewalk out front.

Reese heard her sister's piercing screams and scrambled off her bed. She ran down the stairs two at a time. Their mother, preoccupied with Tracey, did not see Reese run to the kitchen to grab the broomstick hidden behind the icebox.

"Get behind me." Reese looked at her frightened sister trembling in the corner. "Get behind me!" This time her words were crisper and more authoritative.

Tracey obeyed the command and crawled behind Reese for protection.

"You little heifer . . . I could break that damn broom across your fuckin' back."

Reese watched as spit sprayed out of her mother's mouth. Her self-assurance fading, she let the broom rest nervously on her left shoulder.

"Put that damn broom down now! I ain't gonna tell you again . . . and get your fast ass back upstairs. This is between me and your stupid-ass sister."

"But she didn't do nothin'." Reese's words matched her timid stance.

"I told her not to get nothin' out of the icebox, and she ate my damn chicken and now look, she spilt this shit—Wait. Why am I explainin' myself to you?" She put her hands on her hips, the brown leather belt dangling by her side.

"Momma, she was hungry. She didn't mean to—"

"Shut the fuck up!"

Reese knew by the way her mother's lip folded under her teeth and the strength of the word *fuck* that her anger was beyond reasoning. Her mother's use of the word accompanied either cruel beatings or intimate moments with her numerous male friends. Reese knew it was the former.

She took two steps forward. "I'm gonna beat that heifer after I beat the daylights out of you."

Reese stepped back and lifted the broom off of

her shoulder, inches above her head. She swung the broom in her mother's direction, swiping her lightly with the straw end.

"You know your ass is mines." Their mother raised her left arm behind her head.

Reese heard the wisp of the belt in the air before it struck her across the face, inches below her eye. She heard the wisp again and immediately dropped to the floor, sheltering her little sister with her body.

"You bitch!"

Reese tensed her body in preparation for the next session of blows.

Interrupted by a knock on the window, their mother stopped dead and dropped the belt. An older male she had met earlier in the day motioned for her to come outside. She straightened her blouse, patted down her uncombed hair, and cracked open the door. "Give me a minute, Leroy," she said, her voice soft and inviting.

Reese wasn't surprised by her mother's change of demeanor; there were two things she craved—alcohol and men.

As she searched the room for her purse, her cold, dark eyes landed back on Reese and Tracey hovering in the same spot. "Get up and clean up your room," she said under her teeth, not wanting to create a scene in front of company.

Without invitation, Leroy stepped inside the house, landing directly in the living room. He smiled as Reese rose to her feet, until he noticed the blood streaming down her face. His eyes traveled to Tracey, and he saw the thin trickle of blood moving down her arm. His eyes moved upward to their mother. "What are you doing to those two—?"

She threw up her hand. "They're my business," she said. "Mind yours."

"Whatever. Just hurry up." Leroy watched Reese walk past him and pull Tracey by the hand. He wanted to show them a warm smile, something to demonstrate his sympathies, but the two never looked up.

"Let's go." She grabbed her purse and walked towards the door.

"Ain't you gonna change clothes? I mean, you're dirty." Leroy pointed up and down at the many stains on her blouse and pants.

"Why change clothes when they're coming off anyway?"

As Reese got to the top of the stairs leading to the second floor, she heard the door close. Her feeling of relief was immediate, but Tracey was still trembling from the episode. Reese looked directly into Tracey's eyes. "Look, it's gonna be all right. I'll always be here to protect you, okay? It's gonna be all right." Reese turned her shaken sister in her arms and held her tight.

"You promised," Tracey said, her voice barely above a whisper.

"Promised what?"

"Promised to always protect me."

Reese grabbed her sister tighter. "I promise, Tracey. I promise you."

Tracey, feeling strength in her sister's arms and words, stopped crying.

Chapter One

Standing on the corner of 51st and Halsted, Reese studied the decaying community she once called home—Englewood. Five long exhausting years had passed since she last stood in front of Ole Manny Liquor Store, where the stench of piss, rotten garbage, and hopelessness polluted the air. Reese was surprised to see the Ole Manny Liquor Store still in operation. The owner was notorious for selling days-old bread, expired milk, rotten meat, and liquor to underage minors. Reese recalled Ole Manny himself, a fragile, wrinkled Italian man, who looked like death would snatch his last breath at any moment. She remembered her fear when she looked in his charcoal-black eyes. She thought she saw deep-seated evil.

Ole Manny never apologized for selling for profit whatever his patrons desired. If they asked for a single cigarette, he charged a quarter. A can of beer sold for three bucks. Ole Manny even tried to sell the young girls in the neighborhood to the old men who hungered for underdeveloped bodies.

Reese fought back the temptation to peek inside to see if Ole Manny was still bent over the counter, his mouth foaming at the young girls who entered his store to buy Now and Later, or flamin' hot potato chips. Reese recalled how she quickly learned that she could get money by allowing men like Ole Manny to get their freak on with a quick stroke up her inner thigh, or a squeeze on her developing breast, or a feel between the crack of her panties.

Ole Manny showed her favoritism among her classmates. When they entered his store after school to buy candy, pop, and other junk food prohibited at home, Reese always managed to get a bag full of junk food free.

In Reese's home there were no rules. Her mother never cared what time her beloved daughters came strolling through the door. No one questioned her about whether or not she completed her homework, or how her day had progressed. Reese's home was not filled with the aroma of food cooking at dinnertime. Instead, the stench of liquor bottles was as common as the lack of toilet paper.

As early as 11 years old, Reese was very familiar with the taste of Boone's Farm, vodka, and gin. Now 23, the taste of cheap liquor still lingered in her stomach and inside the corners of her mouth.

Reese took a few deep breaths, managing to exhale the bad memories of her childhood, but adolescence and young adulthood would prove to be more difficult. As she turned away from Ole Manny's, a gold four-door Chrysler 300M whirled past her, interrupting her daydream, propelling her to the very last day she was in Chicago. The last day that Tyrell Porter was alive. She shook her head to prevent herself from re-visiting the memories; it was as if she had no control—the car, the store, the stench triggered memories of things she wanted to forget.

She glanced down at her watch. It was close to 6:00 p.m. The busy sidewalks were laden with senior citizens on their regimented walks, students, and the working class going about their day, but it was as though Englewood wore different faces. The rhythm of their walk, the beat of anxious footsteps trying to get to their burglary-proofed homes and deadbolt locks, marked the fading magic.

Another face of the community showed the junkies, drug dealers, troublemakers, and naïve souls fascinated with the darkness. Reese was fascinated with the darkness; that's when her mother left the house, disappearing when the light faded from the sky and re-appearing in the early-morning hours before the sun was fully awake.

Reese studied the crowd of strangers that passed her on their way to their destinations, stern, blank looks plastered on their faces, seeing but not seeing, lost in his or her own drama.

One young girl caught her attention. Wearing a dingy sweatshirt three sizes too big that hung just below her knees, and mismatched jogging pants covered with dirty stains, the girl scratched her arms excessively until thin lines of blood formed. She was begging for change.

Reese could see the disapproving look on the strangers as they sidestepped to avoid the girl. She walked towards Reese as though they knew each other. Reese knew of her pain and of her cravings and reached into her pants pocket to retrieve some change.

The young girl looked down at the coins in her hand. "Is that it? Here,"—She threw the change back at Reese—"this ain't shit! I can't buy no damn liquor with forty-five cents. You got a dollar?"

Reese bit her lip, refusing to allow the laundry list of obscenities to leave her mouth. As she kneeled down to retrieve the change tossed to the concrete, a group of young men emerged from the store. Reese rose with her back turned to the group of young men.

"That bitch was five dollars short with my money," one of the young men complained.

"You ought to knock her stupid ass out. Isn't that the second time she played you?" another asked. "You too soft with the hoes, D. I would have pimp-slapped that trick and sent that ho to the emergency room with a broken-ass neck, even if she was a nickel short. Fuck that—don't play with my money."

Reese cringed at the comment. Her legs grew instantly weak, but she managed to dash across the street, begging not to be recognized. Her three-inch stilettos and the fast pace of the moving cars made her evasion difficult. Cars blared their horns as she tried to sprint to safety. She pulled the hood of her jacket over her head to shield her identity.

"J, I hear you, man. I'm gonna—" The young man stopped mid-sentence when he saw his friend's attention focused on the young lady crossing the street. "That bitch is pigeon-toed as hell." He laughed and pointed at Reese.

"Yeah, she is," Jamal said. "Almost got her ass hit.

Damn, that broad looks familiar as hell." He paused, trying to place her. Her walk sparked his memory.

Reese continued to walk westbound down 51st towards Green Avenue. She held her breath, afraid that just the scent of her breath could arouse Jamal's attention. "Stop it with this crazy shit," she said to herself as she turned the corner, further distancing herself. "He couldn't have recognized you, stupid."

Jamal Winters—The memory of his name made Reese's lip twist up with rage. *That muthafucka.* She gave herself permission to call him the name that she was fearful of saying just minutes before. Reese knew it was inevitable their paths would collide, for this was the second reason for her return to Chicago, her primary reason being Tracey Clark, the beloved sister she'd abandoned for Jamal Winters five years ago.

Five years ago, 18-year-old Reese was barely 110 pounds soaking wet, fully clothed in whatever she found in the trash. She slept on dirty floors of abandoned buildings or in the back seat of deserted cars. She stole for Jamal and did whatever he asked, including being an accessory to murder. As compensation, Jamal kept Reese drugged up and strung out. Reese loved Jamal back then, and she thought Jamal loved her, until he started messing around with her younger sister, Tracey.

Reese continued to walk down Green Avenue, past familiar sights that she wished she could forever burn from her memory. Her life story was a chronic tale of pain and suffering. *Why in the hell did I come back here?*

Her counselor's words stayed with her—"Tracey

is all you have."—motivating her to do what she had to do—find her sister and make amends.

Jamal, confident he knew the identity of the female he'd just seen dodging cars, jumped into his SUV, leaving his boys standing on the corner, scratching their heads in front of Ole Manny Liquor Store. He made a quick U-turn on 51st and turned onto Green Avenue. He spotted Reese walking ahead slowly, as though looking for something or someone. It had been five years, but he could tell just by the hoochie's walk that it was Reese Clark. He continued to nurse on his beer nestled between his legs as he contemplated her return. *What's she up to?*

Reese pulled out the letter given to her by her counselor and studied the last known address of her sister. She had learned from Tracey's foster parents that Tracey was living on the streets, drugging and selling her body.

She remembered the counselor saying, "That chile needs help before she wind up dead like her—"

Reese knew that her counselor wanted to say, "Mother."

Veronica Clark, their mother, was neglectful, abusive, uncaring, and a drunk, yet Reese and Tracey loved her dearly. The thought of her mother made Reese's stomach churn, but she was even more nauseated by the image of her sister shadowing her footsteps. Before she turned 15, Reese had dropped out of high school, was addicted to drugs and prostitution, and had developed a juvenile criminal record that she could wrap herself in. And now Tracey was going down a similar path.

Reese looked at the address on the letter and saw that she was standing in front of a vacant lot. The streets were becoming more congested, and the alleys buzzed with activity. Reese was amused as she watched the children jumping on discarded mattresses. She thought about asking someone if they knew Tracey but decided against it. She continued to walk down the street, cutting through an alley.

"Hey, baby, how much you asking, with yo' f-f-f-fine ass?" a man stationed at a garbage can with his cronies asked. "I got a c-c-couple of dollars." He pulled his pants pockets out.

"I ain't down with that." Reese walked past the group.

"What the f-f-fuck you here f-f-fo' if you ain't with having a good t-t-time?" He grabbed Reese's arm.

Alarm bells set off in her head as the men ogled her with lust in their eyes. She quickly surveyed the surroundings, looking for exit routes, and cursed herself for being stupid enough to use an alley as a shortcut. If she broke free of his hold, her only option was to jump a fence into someone's backyard. She kicked off her shoes.

"Man, she look too clean. She might be a cop," one of the men stated with a hint of panic.

The man released Reese's arm. "I wasn't going t-t-to do nothing."

Reese quickly grabbed her bag and walked backward from the group, her eyes fixed on them. As she continued down the alleyway and approached what appeared to be an abandoned garage, she heard loud moaning and groaning. She peeped through the cracked door and spotted a young girl on her knees in front of a well-dressed man, his dick in her mouth.

"Tracey!" Reese screamed from behind the garage door. She ran to the garage door entrance. "Tracey!" she yelled again, startling her sister, who bit down on the man's penis.

"Aaaaagh, gotdamn bitch." The man pulled his penis out of Tracey's mouth.

"Tracey!" Reese repeated. "It's me, Reese, yo' sister." Reese was about to go over and hug her sister when, suddenly, she felt the steel barrel of a gun in the back of her head.

"Look who's back on the block," Jamal said.

Chapter Two

Carmichael shuffled through several sports magazines, admiring the physiques of the male and female models that danced on the pages. One of the female models had features that resembled Reese. Carmichael growled at the photo. *Reese . . . that bitch.* Nevertheless, Carmichael found himself staring at the photo and feeling an erection protruding through his pants. *Everything she said was a muthafuckin' lie.* Carmichael felt his blood boil. The girl he'd allowed to move into his apartment and deplete his meager bank account was not Lisa Thomas, but Reese Clark.

I should kill that heifer, he thought to himself. As he flipped through the pages of the sports magazine, Carmichael found himself slobbering over the sculpted arms, chiseled abdomen, and muscular legs of a male model. He wished that he could suppress his attraction for men, but a defined body, male or female, always aroused him.

He'd tried to keep his attraction for men under cover, but Reese found out about his dirty secret and exposed him. Carmichael thought he was in love with Reese and was willing to forgive the lies she'd told and even give up the men that he kept in the closet. He would've done anything to keep a life with her. But she stabbed him in the heart when she admitted that she'd never loved him.

It's always bitches with the drama. Men don't carry on like this. You should . . . Carmichael smirked at his incomplete thought. He knew that pussy was too good to settle solely for just dick. Not in this lifetime.

The pressure of his arousal made Carmichael look around the doctor's office for the nearby washroom facilities. He rolled up the magazine in his left hand and rose from his chair to walk across the hallway towards the bathroom.

"Mr. Jones," the nurse said, "Dr. Andrews will see you now."

"Damn." Carmichael tossed the magazine back on the table and followed the nurse through the double doors that separated the waiting area from the examination room.

"Please go in Room 21," the nurse instructed.

To Carmichael's surprise, Dr. Andrews was already in the room when he walked through the door. "Hey, doc," Carmichael said nervously. He sat on the examination table and began to unbutton his shirt.

"No, no, Mr. Jones," the doctor said, "there's no need to get undressed. I won't be examining you today, but"—He glanced down at the chart on his lap—"we need to discuss your test results."

A stoic look on his face, Carmichael tried to read the doctor's expression. He released an anxious laugh. "What up, doc? What cha find? Give it to me straight. I bet it's sugar. Yeah, I bet that's why I'm tired all the time," he rambled on. "Sugar runs in my family—my momma, my poppa, his folks— hell, everyone I can think of. But I heard there's medication." He lowered his voice. "Stops a man from getting it up. Doc, I'm 54 years old, and I still . . . you know what I'm talking about." Carmichael laughed.

The doctor continued to look at Carmichael. His serious face told Carmichael that sugar wasn't the problem.

"That's it, isn't it?"

The doctor coughed to clear his throat. "Maybe we should request that the social worker come in here for support."

"I don't want no damn social worker. Tell me."

"Okay, you're partially correct. You have been diagnosed with hypertension, which may require medication. However, you have also been diagnosed with chlamydia. It's a sexually transmitted—"

"That dirty bitch gave me what?" Carmichael jumped off the examination table.

"Please, Mr. Jones, I need for you to calm down."

Carmichael sat back down.

"I know this is disturbing news to receive, but I would like the names of your sexual partners so that we may—"

"I ain't telling you shit." Carmichael jumped off the examination table again and walked towards the door.

"Please, Mr. Jones, settle down so that I can give you the information you need for treatment."

"Fuck that treatment! I ain't doing shit." He yanked open the door.

The nurse walked towards the room. "Is everything okay, Mr. Jones?"

"What the fuck you looking at?" Carmichael said, leaving the nurse standing in front of the examination room.

David Davenport paced back and forth in Terminal A of the Detroit airport, waiting impatiently for his flight to Chicago. The inclement weather in Detroit had flights delayed for several hours, and the setback caused David's anger to fester out of control. He'd submitted his letter of resignation to his boss, thus terminating his relationship with the Detroit Police Department after seven years of exemplary service. His supervisor, initially refusing to accept his resignation, pleaded with David to consider a leave of absence, but David knew that he was on the verge of "crossing the line" and didn't want to hide behind his badge. Proud of the years he'd served as a police officer, David wanted to leave his job with the same dignity and honor that he possessed the first day he took the oath of being a cop. He dropped his letter of resignation on top of his supervisor's desk and exited the office without even a mumbled goodbye.

David retrieved his brother's obituary from his inside coat pocket. He traced the outline of his brother's photo with his pinky finger, and his eyes grew moist. It had been five years since Tyrell's brutal murder in the streets of Chicago, and still no one had been arrested for the crime. For David, justice was delayed long enough.

"Five years, five years, five years," David repeated over and over, his voice increasing in volume, causing nearby passengers to get up from their seats and move away from him. He didn't care about the suspicious eyes that watched him curiously, seeing him as a walking time bomb. He was.

David could still hear the high pitch of his mother's cries when she called that fateful night to inform him that his brother was dead.

"David, oh my God, my God, sweet Jesus, they killed my baby. They killed my baby, sweet Jesus!"

Whoever killed Tyrell also killed their mother, who died six months later from a broken heart. David buried the last family member he had, and now he wanted someone else to feel the pain that he had been dealing with for more than five years.

Tyrell's unsolved murder tarnished David's belief in the judicial system that he vowed to honor and uphold. Tyrell was dismantled and murdered, and the Chicago Police Department put forth little effort to bring his murderer to justice. David knew the attitude all too well; he wore it himself in Detroit. But Tyrell was not just a drug dealer. He was someone's son, brother, and friend.

"I promise I'm going to find your murderer," David said, speaking to the photo. "I found that bitch that you were fucking. Imagine that." He laughed. "That was your muthafuckin' problem, bro—pussy."

David had spoken to Tyrell hours before his death. It was nothing unusual; he generally spoke to

Felicia Madlock

his brother every day. And though their lifestyles were polar opposites—Tyrell sold drugs and David was a cop—they had a boyhood history, a bond of brotherhood that compelled them to keep in touch. They always had something to talk about.

David used his every persuasive skill to get Tyrell out of the drug game. But how do you convince someone to take a $40,000-a-year job when he could flip that in one night? The math just didn't add up.

It's no secret that drug dealers are considered disposable. Society says, "Good riddance," when one of them is killed. But the Chicago police had an obligation to do a thorough investigation.

When the assigned officers refused to give David the status reports on the case, thereby violating the informal code of "cop brotherhood," he suspected a cover-up. And when his brother's case was labeled cold before the dirt was thrown on his body, due to lack of evidence, David, mad as hell, began his own detective work. He began to visit Chicago, making friends with important people, like the janitorial staff, file clerks, and security guards, to obtain whatever information he needed. He was able to obtain a copy of the fingerprint report that identified a wineglass with his brother's prints and those of a female, Reese Clark.

Reese Clark, he learned, had been a girlfriend of Jamal Winters. Jamal, a one-time childhood friend of Tyrell, became a player, just like Tyrell. They eventually became enemies, each working the same game in the same territory. When David learned that Tyrell was last seen entering a building owned by a family member of Jamal Winters, he began to see a

connection. Police chalked up his findings as coinci-
dental, but David felt like he was on to something.
His gut told him that Jamal Winters was behind his
brother's death, but he wanted proof before he pulled
the trigger.

David pulled out several photos of Reese from his
duffle bag. He'd learned she was a junkie, period.
But her most recent picture, taken less than a week
earlier, captured her in a different light. David hated
to admit it, but he found Reese attractive. *That bitch
was involved with your brother's death*, he reminded
himself. *I might have to fuck her before I kill her.* His
thoughts were interrupted by the announcement of
his flight boarding to Chicago.

Chapter Three

Reese stood frozen on the concrete, the steel barrel pressed against her head.

Jamal enjoyed the cold look of fear in her eyes. And when he saw the warm stream of urine puddle on the floor, he smiled. "What the fuck brings you back here?"

"I-I-I came back . . . I-I came back for Tracey."

Tracey got up from her knees and dusted the dirt off her pants. She studied Reese clearly for the first time. "Shoot that bitch," Tracey said. "Give me the gun. I'll shoot her my damn self."

Jamal pushed Tracey away as she tried to grab the gun.

Tracey pointed her finger in Reese's face. "You came back for who, bitch?" she asked, standing inches away from her.

"For you," Reese whispered. "I'm sorry."

"You damn right, you're a sorry ass. I haven't seen you in over five years. Yo' ass just left, up and gone without saying a word, and now you're back? As far as I'm concerned, you could have stayed gone, stayed dead."

Jamal laughed at the interchange and lowered his gun. "Now this some shit you see on Jerry Springer. You want to shoot her?" He offered the gun to Tracey.

Tracey's right eyebrow perched up, as though she was interested. She snatched the gun from Jamal's hand and waved it in Reese's face.

"Bitch, don't snatch nothing from me," he said, taking the gun back.

"I didn't mean—"

"I don't give a fuck what you didn't mean." The harshness in his voice caused Tracey to retreat.

He turned to Reese. His words came out as pure silk. "What you been doing in Detroit?"

"Nothing," Reese said nervously. "Nothing at all."

"You're a muthafuckin' liar." Tracey walked up to Reese and slapped her in the face. "Jamal told me that yo' ass was up there ho'in', druggin', and shit."

"Yeah, Reese, you could have stayed in Chi-town fo' that shit. But . . . mmm . . . lemme look at you— You finally got an ass, girl." Jamal slapped her on the rear. "I could get a premium dollar for you. Yo' sister nothin' but a two-dollar dick-suckin' tramp."

Reese saw the hurt in Tracey's eyes. "I'm not down for that no more, Jamal. I'm not druggin' either."

"Good for you." He clapped. "You shoulda told a nigga you was comin'. I could have had you set up somewhere."

"That's okay. I was hoping that I could stay with Tracey."

"Tracey?" He started to laugh again. "That bitch don't have a fuckin' pot to piss in. She doin' the same damn thing you did—sleepin' wherever, you know."

"I got a place. You know that."

"Oh yeah, that's right. Your ass stay in that fuckin' rathole at the Lincoln Hotel."

"It's mines." Tracey pouted.

"Whatever, bitch!"

"I'm out of here." Tracey exited the garage and didn't look back.

"Tracey! Tracey, don't leave yet." Jamal tucked his gun back in his pants.

Reese exhaled a breath of relief.

Jamal looked at her and chuckled. "We ain't finish," he replied as though he were reading her mind. "You comin' with me."

Jamal drove Reese around Englewood, passing familiar places, places where they once hung out. They just drove. No words were exchanged.

From time to time Reese glanced at Jamal from the corner of her eye, each quick look reminding her how much she had grown to hate him.

"Where we goin'?"

"Where you want to go?" He reached over and caressed Reese's upper thigh.

She wanted to smack it away but feared his reaction.

Jamal descended on the Dan Ryan Expressway heading south. His deceptively calm, obliging attitude frightened her.

He turned up the volume on his radio, allowing

The Game's "Hate It or Leave It" to fill the air. He rapped along with the song, occasionally peeping over at Reese. "I usually kill a muthafucka that disobeys my orders. I told you never to come back, but—"

"I'm sorry. I'm really sorry. I didn't mean to disobey, but Tracey's the only family I got. I simply wanted her to—" Reese stopped mid-sentence when she read the signs on the expressway—NEXT EXIT JOLIET, ILLINOIS—and became more concerned for her safety.

Jamal took the Joliet exit and drove onto a service road that lead to a dingy, run-down diner that had a parking lot filled with 18-wheeler trucks. He pulled in a vacant parking spot and turned off the car engine.

"You know, I could make a fortune here with your fine ass." Jamal turned on the interior light and looked directly at Reese. "These truck drivers, they need some ass."

"Please, Jamal . . . I ain't like that no more, truly. I'm trying to get my life together."

"And you want to fuck Tracey's life up, right?"

"No, I don't."

"Shut the fuck up! You hungry?"

Reese did not answer.

He exited the automobile and looked at Reese sternly. He directed her to follow him inside the diner. She rubbed her sweaty palms together, not knowing what was to come next.

As the two entered the poorly lit diner, a sea of anonymous faces turned around to watch. Jamal walked over to an empty booth. "Whatcha want to eat?" He bounced up and down on the worn bench.

"I'm not hungry," Reese lied, her stomach growling for food.

"Not hungry, huh. Well, your ass can starve. I'm getting something." He took a quick look at the menu. "I guess I'll stick with my usual sloppy burger and a vanilla shake. What the hell you want?"

"I'm not hungry."

"Suit yourself." He signaled for the waitress.

"Hey, baby." The waitress pulled out her tablet to take their order.

Reese cringed when she saw the waitress was missing her top row of teeth.

"Hey, Charlene, you know me. I'm getting the usual. Make that to go."

"And you, young lady?" she asked, watching Reese bite on the nail of her thumb. "Our food tastes better than yo' finger, chile." She laughed.

"I'm not hungry."

"You sure?" The waitress looked at Jamal for reassurance.

"Let her ass starve."

"Jamal! Baby, do you at least want something to drink then?"

"Yeah, a Coke." Reese continued to bite her nails.

"I'll be right with you," Charlene said to another patron sitting across from Jamal and Reese.

Jamal bent over the table towards Reese. "I'm asking you for the last damn time. Do you—"

"I said I ain't hungry," she replied through clenched teeth.

"Fine." He threw his hands in the air. "That's it, Charlene."

Charlene wrote down their order on the tablet, winked at Jamal, and walked away.

Jamal tapped his finger impatiently on the table and stared at Reese. She tried to ignore his watchful eyes, glancing instead at the customers in the restaurant.

"You must come here often, right?"

"How so?"

"You and Charlene seem to know each other."

"Yeah, you might say so. She's my godmother. We still watch out for each other."

"Oh." Reese went back to chewing her nails.

Reese felt her purse vibrating and excused herself to go to the washroom. When she opened the door to the women's bathroom, the stench of the urinals quickly assaulted her. She thought about holding her bladder but wasn't sure when she would have another chance to go to the bathroom, and her sides were in excruciating pain. She pushed open one stall door and found the toilet running over with shit and toilet paper. The second stall was in a similar condition, just not overflowing. She squatted over the second urinal and took care of her business.

After she finished washing her hands, she checked the messages on her cell phone. She saw that she had seven messages and seven missed calls. She dialed the last number.

"Where in the hell are you?"

"Everything is as planned," she explained.

"How is 'everything is as planned'? I don't know where the fuck you are."

"I made contact with Jamal. I'm with him now. That muthafucka is—" Reese quickly terminated the conversation when Charlene walked through the door of the bathroom.

Jamal paid for his food, left Charlene a generous

tip, and waited impatiently for Reese by the diner's entrance.

Charlene exited the washroom facility first and looked in Jamal's direction. She signaled him with her eyes to wait, but he read her wrong and gave a swift wave. In her haste to get to him, she knocked over a customer's beer.

"You clumsy-ass broad," the male patron shouted.

"I'm sorry. I'm so sorry. Let me go get some more napkins."

When Charlene looked up, Jamal and Reese had already exited. She ran out the front door and into the parking lot, only to see the SUV driving off. She made a mental note to call Jamal as soon as she got off work then walked back into the diner to deal with the disgruntled customer.

Jamal drove off the service road near the highway onto Hennepin Boulevard. He pulled into an abandoned gas station. Confused, Reese looked at him but didn't question his actions.

He spent a few minutes fiddling with the radio before directing his attention to her. "I got business to take care of." He leaned closer to Reese, grabbed her by the neck, and pulled her towards him for a kiss, his hand roaming underneath her shirt.

Repulsed by his sexual gestures, Reese initially wanted to pull away but decided that it would be better to go along with "the game." Her body grew stiff when Jamal placed her hand on his erect penis.

Their encounter ended abruptly when lights flashed in their rear window. Jamal jumped, and Reese sighed with relief.

"Shit," Jamal muttered under his breath. He

peeped in his rearview mirror, fearing that the flashing lights were from an approaching police car. "Oh, that's my brother, Jun-Jun." Jamal started up his SUV and pulled out of the gas station behind the old Ford Mustang.

Reese straightened her clothes.

"We will resume our business later." Jamal followed the Mustang through the unfamiliar streets of Joliet. They drove up and down residential blocks.

Reese remained silent as she alternately watched Jamal and the streets. She recognized that familiar nervous twitch and excessive shaking of his leg that always appeared when something serious was on his mind. His posture in his SUV was alert and erect. *Something big is about to happen.*

"I should put your ass out," he mumbled. "You don't need to see or be a part of . . ." He paused. "Mmmmm." He snapped his finger while slowing down for a stop sign. "On second thought, you might come in handy."

Reese kept her attention fixed on the houses in the neighborhood. She saw shadows moving behind sheer curtains and tried to guess about the types of lives the residents led, wondering if anyone had an upbringing more horrible than hers.

Jamal finally parked behind the Mustang at the end of a deserted residential block, and began making calls on his cell phone. He would occasionally catch Reese looking at him. He'd then wink at her and seductively lick his lips.

She simply rolled her eyes and gazed back into the darkness.

"Get the fuck out! Hurry!" Jamal flung twenty

dollars on her lap. "I decided I don't need for you to be here when—look, get yourself a cab, get on the bus, fuckin' hitch or somethin', but get the hell out of my ride."

"Jamal, baby, please . . ." Reese looked around the SUV. "I don't know where I'm at. Please, at least take me to—"

"I ain't takin' you nowhere. I got business to take care of."

"I won't be in the way. Promise I won't be."

"Shut the fuck up, wouldja!"

Jamal answered his phone. "Yeah, muthafucka, we here. Everything straight. Where the fuck are you? Hurry up!"

Just then, loud screeching tires from a motor-cycle came from the opposite direction. The motor-cycle slowed down as it approached Jamal's SUV and stopped in front of Jun-Jun's Mustang.

Within seconds, thunderous gunshots were fired in the Ford Mustang. Jamal screamed, unleashing his own volley of gunshots at the motorcycle, which sped away from the scene.

Jamal and Reese ran over to the driver's side of the Mustang, where Jun-Jun lay dead, blood splat-tered on the front seat and dashboard, and shattered glass everywhere. Porch lights from nearby homes flicked on, and residents began stepping out onto their porches.

Jamal grabbed Reese by the arm. "We gotta get outta here," he said as the police sirens speedily ap-proached.

"Deja vu," Reese said to herself, jumping into his SUV.

Chapter Four

Carmichael exited the medical complex in a blinding rage. "Outta my way," he growled to anyone remotely in his path.

"I don't have that shit," he yelled back at the medical building, shaking his fist in denial. "I don't got it."

Once in his car, he reached under his seat for his silver flask. He tossed his head back and emptied the Jack Daniel's down his throat like it was Kool-Aid. "Aaaaaaaahhhh . . . that shit is good." Wanting more, Carmichael rummaged through the car, hoping to find a discarded bottle lodged under his seat with even just a swig left for his dry lips. "Shit." He came up empty.

He slammed the gears of his car in reverse, sideswiping the car adjacent to him as he tried to back out of his parking space. "Oh shit." He laughed. "I better get the fuck outta here."

Carmichael drove a few blocks down ML King

Avenue, repeatedly monitoring his rearview mirror for cops. He drove another half-mile before he spotted One Stop Liquor. He parked his car in front of a fire hydrant.

"You can't park your car there, sir," a store employee gathering shopping baskets politely told him.

"Listen, young c-c-c-cat, don't f-f-fuckin' tell me what to do." Carmichael waved the kid off. He stumbled into the liquor store and quickly spotted the Jack Daniel's Black Label. "That's my main man." He grabbed two bottles, tucking one under each arm. He stumbled into a rack of chips, causing it to tumble. "Ooops." He drifted away. Customers in the checkout line laughed at him, but he was oblivious.

Once he reached the front of the line, he retrieved a wet twenty-dollar bill from his pants pocket and handed it to the store clerk. "Here, sweet m-m-momma."

The disgusted store attendee looked at the money. "Sorry, sir, but that'll be $46.36."

Carmichael dug into his pocket for more bills. He brought up a crumpled wad and begrudgingly handed another two twenties across the counter. After the clerk bagged the bottles and handed them over, Carmichael smiled and told her to keep the change. He waved to the customers on his way out, the Jack Daniel's snuggled close to his heart.

He got in his car and turned up the first bottle to his lips. "Aaaaaahhhhh." He licked the rim. He inserted his keys into the ignition and sped out of his illegal parking spot, straight into the traffic. He didn't check his side mirror; he didn't see the 18-wheeler bearing down on him.

The truck driver blared his horn and reached for his brakes, but at 45 miles per hour, he knew he was in trouble. The truck slammed into the rear of Carmichael's car, causing him to enter a second line of traffic, where his car was struck again. The 18-wheeler jackknifed, and Carmichael's car careened out of control onto a grassy median that separated north-south traffic.

Brakes, horns, and screams brought onlookers into the area. The One Stop store clerk ran to Carmichael's car. "Call the paramedics," she shouted when she saw Carmichael's body pinned behind the steering wheel, his head slung back and blood dripping profusely from both sides. The clerk tried to open both front doors, but the impact of the collision left them jammed. Carmichael's front seat was knocked out of its place, the driver's side door was folded in, and the jagged metal was cutting into Carmichael's body.

"Call the paramedics," the clerk shouted again, looking for any sign of life.

"Is he okay?" one of the onlookers asked.

"I don't know. I don't think so."

"What happened?" another person asked.

Now, all the voices were shouting orders, asking questions, making comments.

Someone pointed. "That lady over there was ejected from her car. She's dead. I just know it."

"But her baby was in the back seat and only received a few scratches. Thank God," another person added.

"He was drunk," the store clerk said matter-offactly. "All I know is that he got in his car and got run over by that 18-wheeler."

A mass of arms started waving when the crowd spotted the paramedics. "Over here! Over here!" they shouted.

The owner of One Stop Liquor raced out of his store towards the clerk. "What happened?"

The store employee only shook her head.

Chapter Five

David drove around the once-familiar streets of Chicago, fondly remembered as the low end of town. But communities like the Gap, Bonneville, Washington Park, and Kenwood were getting a facelift. These areas, known for their high crime rate, grinding poverty, and double-digit unemployment had suddenly changed from ghetto dwellings to ghetto fabulous, with one-bedroom condos starting at $200,000. David counted the new rehab projects as he drove along Drexel Boulevard and Cottage Grove.

Gentrification is alive and thriving. He drove southbound towards 63rd Street and eastbound towards Lake Shore Drive, finally pulling up to the Hayes Drive entrance near the recreational facility. He exited his vehicle and walked towards the basketball courts, hoping to catch a few minutes of a lively game before his appointment.

The young males dominating the court ran up

and down with the energy that only youth could provide. David reminisced about the countless times he'd played with his brother Tyrell. The memories overwhelmed him, bringing tears to the corners of his eyes. "Man up, man up," he told himself.

He turned his attention back to the game and felt a pinch of jealousy for the agility the young men displayed on the court. He laughed.

Barely 37, David knew that society still viewed him as a young man, but the death of his brother and mother within the same year aged him considerably. His life, once fulfilling, was now a long, dull quest to satisfy his vengeful rage against those responsible for his brother's murder. He consoled himself that he'd tried to follow the law, but lack of justice denied him closure. In David Davenport's world, the murder of Tyrell Porter was front page news, though his death barely garnered three lines in the community newspaper. It was the events surrounding his brother's murder that kept David's blood warm and his mind focused on his ultimate goal.

Money brought him snippets of information that he managed to piece together over the years, but he hit the jackpot when his path crossed Tracey Clark's— Reese Clark's younger sister and Jamal's baby mama. They met when she needed money or had some information to sell. She named the locations for the meetings, usually a neighborhood hole in the wall where the patrons stayed too drunk to care about the coming and going of any new face. He didn't complain; he enjoyed the anonymity. He was surprised this time, when she suggested meeting at the lakefront, an open and visible spot.

It took David a while to gain Tracey's trust, but money and drugs could buy the devil's soul if it's the right price. They formed a simple allegiance—he gave her money; she gave him information. David would later learn that Tracey had an agenda, that she hated Reese as much as he did, maybe more.

His diabolical mind often thought of setting Tracey up for the murders that would transpire once he set his plan in action, but he wanted to believe he still had standards, lines he wouldn't cross. Nothing so far had led him to believe she'd played any part in his brother's murder. He knew in his gut that Jamal and Reese were tied in, but he needed the full story. Anyone, everyone involved needed to pay.

He glanced down at his watch a fourth time. Tracey was over an hour late.

What the fuck! She's always late. He had been meeting with her for over a year and couldn't ever recall her being on time. David felt like he was working for her, not the other way around.

Becoming increasingly impatient, David started to walk towards his car, until he heard his name called out. He turned and saw Tracey waving frantically, running in his direction. Her appearance alarmed him. Her hair was uncombed, and she wore a long man's shirt that draped on her skinny body like a dress. He looked embarrassed for her, and for himself to be seen with her in public.

"David, David," she yelled, "wait up. Don't leave." Winded from the run, but genuinely happy to see him, she attempted to give him a hug.

He reluctantly patted her on her back and re- moved himself from her embrace. "You're late," he said angrily. "I can't be waiting for yo' ass to come when you good and ready."

"Yeah, yeah," she replied nonchalantly. "I got some news for yo' ass. And this will cost you plenty, baby . . . extra."

"I know," he said sarcastically. "Reese is in Chicago. Please do not go and get cocky. I'm a cop—" David stopped, realizing what he'd said.

"A cop?"

"I'm not a cop. I used to be, but that ain't got nothin' to do with nothin', trust me."

"Why you payin' me all this money for information on my sister?" Tracey's serious eyes pierced his.

David had to think quickly. He'd never explained to her why he needed to know about Reese. Perhaps this was the time.

As he opened his mouth to speak, she laughed and blurted out, "Oh well, fuck that! I don't care. Just keep paying me. You could kill her, for all I care."

Chapter Six

"Wha' muthafucka killed my brother?" Jamal smacked a young male in the mouth with the butt of his gun.

The young man gagged, coughing up blood.

"Ease up, J," another male said from the background.

"Fuck you," Jamal shouted over his shoulder, "or I'll pistol whip your bitch ass too."

Jamal bent in close to the injured man and listened to his erratic breathing. "Muthafucka!" He shoved the gun in the young man's face. "Whada they call you?"

"Huh?"

"Your name. What's your name?"

"Shaun."

"Shaun, I'm going to give you one last chance to tell me who killed my brother."

"I don't know," the young man whimpered. He sat in the chair, his hands bound behind him, blood dripping down the corner of his mouth onto his torn shirt. His eyes followed Jamal's pacing back and forth in front of him. He cringed every time Jamal stopped to glare at him.

Jamal shouted, "Darren, what you hear on the streets?"

"Nothing, J, not a peep." Darren shrugged his shoulders. "Nobody's saying nothing. I don't think the Cobras got shit to do with it."

"And who appointed your dumb ass the mutha-fuckin' judge and jury?" Jamal now pointed the gun at Darren.

"I'm just saying—" Darren replied.

"I didn't ask you to say shit." Jamal's eyes narrowed to slits and turned again to the victim in the chair. Pointing his finger close to his face, he said, "I can smell guilty on his dirty ass." He slammed the gun again into the young man's jaw, taking him by surprise.

"Jamal!" Darren grabbed Jamal's arm. "Look, man, I could care less about this stupid-ass busta, but do you want this type of heat on us? Now? We don't need the heat of CPD riding our asses over this bullshit."

"So my brother's killing is bullshit?"

"Naw, J, you know that ain't what I'm saying. We gon' find the muthafuckas that gunned down Jun-Jun."

Jamal focused his attention back on the young man bound in the chair. "Okay, muthafucka, did you or some of yo' boys kill my brother?" Jamal lowered his gun and his voice and stared at the young man, who was now trying to gather strength to answer the question. Jamal pulled a milk crate up to the young man and spoke directly into his face. "Well?"

The young man shook his head no.

Darren knew from experience that once Jamal lowered his voice he was getting ready to do something violent. "Whadya gonna do with him?"

"This dead muthafucka here?" Jamal rose, pointed his gun at the young man's head, and pulled the trigger. "That's what."

Chapter Seven

"Tracey, Tracey," Reese yelled when she spotted her sister walking on the opposite side of the street. She waved her hands frantically to get her attention.

Tracey heard Reese calling her name but chose to ignore her.

Reese sprinted across the street and down the block to catch up with her sister, about to enter a dilapidated building.

"Tracey, wait, dammit." Reese was out of breath. She held her hand on the door, preventing Tracey from going inside the reddish-brown structure, which looked ready to be condemned. Several of the front windows were boarded up, but the Lincoln Hotel sign continued to blink on and off, its vacancy sign lit up.

"Tracey, stop. Shit! We need to talk."

"Fuck you, Reese. Take your ass back to dirty Detroit. I don't need you."

A man leaving the building joked, "Can I go with ya?"

"Fuck you," Tracey said to the old man.

"Okay, when? Here?" He started to unbuckle his belt. He then unzipped his pants, exposing his soft, wrinkled penis.

Tracey appeared unfazed by the old man's attempt at humor.

Reese gasped. "He don't have on underwear, Tracey."

"No shit." Tracey walked the long corridor to her room, and Reese followed, all the while trying not to rub against the grimy, feces-smeared, roach-infested walls.

"We need to talk," Reese repeated.

"We don't have shit to talk about. Damn!" Tracey inserted her key into the door. "Jamal should have shot your ass in the mouth when he had the chance."

Reese followed Tracey into her one-room apartment and was saddened by the shabby conditions. "I wanted to tell you why I came back."

"I don't give a flyin' fuck why you came back."

"I know it's hard for you to believe, but I did come back for you, Tracey. My counselor got in touch with your foster parents. They said they tried to help you as much as they could. They tried to prevent you from seeing Jamal, but you got pregnant and—"

"Yeah, whatever. Fuck them and you, Reese. Everybody wanna help poor Tracey, but they don't care. They got what they really wanted. They took Jabaree from me."

"Look, Tracey, I'm trying to tell you that I'm sorry, okay? I'm sorry for everything."

"You's a muthafuckin' lyin' bitch." Tracey walked to face Reese. "You never cared about me. You only cared about Jamal, and it made you sick to think that we hooked up and I had his son."

"Do you at least visit Jabaree?"

"None of your goddamn business." Tracey sat back on her bed. She started scratching her arms and twitching legs.

"Look at you . . . you can't keep still for a minute. That shit gots you fucked up. Jamal gots you fucked up. Tracey, you know I've been there. Remember?" Reese walked to where Tracey sat on the bed and dropped to her knees. She enclosed Tracey's hands into hers. "Sis, I'm sorry for leaving you, but I was too messed up to help anyone. I left for Detroit doing the same dirt I was doing here in Chicago. I was beyond fucked up, but at some point I got help. I was assigned a counselor, and she forced me to see that I was going down the same path as Ma." Tears started to form in Reese's eyes. "I mean, Ma abandoned us, I left you, and I'm sorry. But I'm back. Unlike Ma, I cleaned up, partially for you."

"Reese, feed that bowl of shit to someone else. You been gone for five fuckin' years. You didn't even say goodbye. I knew that yo' stupid ass was in Detroit suckin' dick, and you goin' to help me? Ha! What a joke."

"Tracey, everything you said is true. It was foul how I left, but I didn't want to leave, word to my God."

"Then why did ya?"

"I can't say," Reese said between clenched teeth, remembering her conversation with Jamal.

"You're a muthafuckin' liar. I'm so tired of your shit. Jamal said—"

"Jamal? You can't believe one word of what he says. He don't give a damn about no one but himself."

"Whatever." Tracey pulled back the soiled cover on her bed to get a bag of wrapped crack cocaine. She broke a piece of the eight ball of cocaine, lifted her pipe from underneath her pillow, and began to fill it with Brillo stuffing. After melting down the piece, she put the pipe to her lips. She winked at Reese, seeing the hunger in her eyes.

The aroma that permeated the room caused Reese to feel faint. Her muscles stiffened, and her lips ached. She wanted to indulge, to feel the freedom that initial hit could give her. Reese quickly got up and moved towards the door, Tracey immediately at her side.

"Don't go, sis." Tracey put the pipe to her sister's lips. "Stay and tell me how you came back to help me."

Reese inhaled and closed her eyes. The bells that she swore she would never hear again were ringing as she filled her lungs.

The nurse entered the hospital room to monitor Carmichael's vital signs. She checked the visitor's log and frowned. No one had visited the unconscious patient. Then she walked out into the hallway toward a group of doctors who were talking about their golf scores.

"Dr. Fletcher, we still don't have a name for this John Doe. I think it's time to get the police involved, to ID him."

"We have. Marlene said that his name is Carmichael Winters. Maybe she hasn't written the info in the chart yet," Dr. Fletcher explained.

"Did she contact any family members or friends?" the nurse asked.

"I don't know. Do you want her pager number so you can follow up with her with these questions?" Dr. Fletcher's reply showed irritation.

"No, it's easier to ask you," she said. "Thanks." The nurse walked into another patient's room.

Chapter Eight

Tracey walked into the darkness, feeling the fatigue of her 48-hour sleeping binge. She noticed her door left slightly ajar. Reese was gone. She laughed when she recalled how Reese held the pipe in her shaking hands, her eyes hungry for the fix. "Yeah, clean. *Dirty* muthafucka, someone needs to help you."

The humid, sweaty night air made Tracey anxious and hungry. She walked up 51st, frowning at the emptiness of the streets. *Where is everyone?* The muscles in her lower calves felt inflamed, and she grunted with each agonizing step.

She walked past Halsted Street westbound toward Morgan Avenue. She decided to take a shortcut through an abandoned lot filled with debris, broken bottles, and a few deserted cars. The house adjoining the lot blared out old-school music from an open second-floor window. She stopped to stare at the silhouettes that danced behind the curtains. Then, leaning against the house, she loosened the painfully tight butterflies on her sneakers, to give her feet breathing room.

She moved to the front of the house and stared at the porch. Its chipped stairs and wobbly banisters made her laugh out loud. She thought about the many times she hurt herself on those damn stairs. She heard her mother's words: "Your clumsy ass is going to break your damn neck. You better watch where you's goin'."

Tracey wished that she could have broken her leg, arm, or something, to get her mother's attention. But her mother's attention was always preoccupied with her many boyfriends and their tormenting tempers. *Odd*, Tracey thought nostalgically, *how I remember the corners of every room where I hovered, trying to stay quiet and out of Mother's way.* Then she recalled the comfort of her sister's arms, always surrounding her, keeping her calm, hushing her, protecting her from their mother's wrath.

Reese was only 9 years old when she assumed her mother's responsibilities. She fed, clothed, and loved Tracey. Tracey idolized her older sister and wasted no time imitating her as she got older. When Reese started smoking, Tracey picked up the habit. Reese started to use drugs, so Tracey indulged. And because Reese loved Jamal's dirty drawers, Tracey needed to love him too.

Their mother stayed away from the house days at a time, and food was scarce. It was Reese that put food in the icebox to quiet their hunger pangs.

When Family Services intervened, they were shifted together from one foster home to another. Tracey measured the foster home according to Reese's likes and dislikes. If Reese ran away, Tracey would eventually follow her, despite how she personally felt about her foster parents.

At the funeral, Tracey couldn't recall seeing the men that frequented her mother's bed, but Reese was by her side. It was Reese who brushed her hair, hugged her, and consoled her. She hung on to Reese's words: "Don't cry, I will always take care of you."

She couldn't understand why she woke up one morning and found her sister's belongings gone. Months and months went by, and Tracey didn't hear a word from Reese—no phone calls, no letters, no messages from a friend of a friend, nothing. Her sadness festered to anger when she discovered that she had to take care of herself. Barely 17 years old and naïve to the ways of the streets, she was given a crash course on survival.

She bent down and picked up a stone and threw it against the porch. "Fuck this shit," she said, sorry to revisit the old memories. They never brought answers.

Tracey walked away, engrossed in the nightmarish tales of her childhood, and accidentally bumped into a male stranger.

"Excuse me," she mumbled.

The man's stench made her pinch her nose. His scruffy beard and matted afro looked like they housed families of maggots. She tried to sidestep him, but he blocked her path.

"Move," she yelled, pushing at his side.

He stood several inches taller than Tracey, but his frame was fragile and certainly not intimidating to her. He grabbed her by the shoulders and flung her around quickly in a chokehold.

She grabbed his arms in a desperate attempt to break his grip, but he was surprisingly strong. She started to scream, but the sharp point at the base of her throat silenced her cries.

He led her at knifepoint to a secluded spot in the alley.

Reese's words echoed in her mind: "Don't worry, I will always care for you."

Tracey glanced down at the man's arm that remained tight around her neck, and saw the track marks. *Damn, if only I had some juice for this muthafucka, maybe he'd—*

Tracey couldn't complete her thought, because her body was suddenly flung to the ground. She scrambled to her feet, but her attacker got on top of her, yanking her hair.

She looked into his eyes, wanting to find compassion, something to give her hope, but the look that came back was dark and empty, devoid of any feelings. Her attacker began banging her head repeatedly against the hard concrete. She allowed her body to go limp, hoping he would sense that she was no longer resisting. The repeated blows on the concrete made Tracey go in and out of consciousness; she hardly felt his penis penetrating her vagina.

Tracey closed her eyes and focused on the warm sensation of blood pouring out of her body. She felt a cold gush of air around her neck; she knew her throat had been slashed. Tracey then started praying to God, asking him to let her die.

Chapter Nine

Charlene nestled back in her oversized La-Z-Boy recliner, a bowl of popcorn in her lap and a six-pack of Miller within arm's length, glad she'd been given two consecutive days off. Two days to do absolutely nothing. She snatched the remote control from a nearby coffee table and hit the play button. She recently purchased Eddie Murphy's *Raw* video from the local Wal-Mart for $1.99 and couldn't wait for a night like this to rip open the plastic and plop in her first DVD in her new DVD player. She wanted to spend a quiet night at home, laughing at her television screen until her sides hurt and her eyes blurred with tears.

As the previews played out on the TV screen, she grabbed her cell phone and placed another call to Carmichael's number. Carmichael, Charlene's second cousin on her mother's side, was also the ex-lover of her deceased friend, Jamella Black.

Again his phone kept ringing.

"Inconsiderate buzzard." She wondered why she even bothered to maintain contact with him, when he was too selfish to return her calls. She couldn't recall the last time she spoke to him, maybe a couple of weeks. *He could be dead and you wouldn't know it.*

Charlene laughed out loud, reminiscing about the "good old days," when they would hang out. Carmichael, a lady's man, had style and strutted about town in his suits, famous for their flamboyant colors of red or yellow. He kept his shoes always polished to a high shine. And every Tuesday he kept his standing appointment for a manicure.

Sweet Jamella was swept away by his smooth talk, but it was his street savvy that made Carmichael attractive to the women. So attractive, in fact, that he fathered many children by many women. Jamella thought he would settle down with the announcement of her pregnancy, but his womanizing didn't stop. He popped in and out of his son's life, as he did with all his other children—at his convenience. He rarely visited Jamella and his son Jamal. Jamella even thought that giving her son Carmichael's last name would create a long-lasting bond, but Carmichael never cared.

Then when Jamella became ill and her health quickly deteriorated, Charlene prayed Carmichael would become more involved, but he simply dropped cash on her kitchen table and went about his business. As godmother to Jamal, Charlene felt she had to intervene. She berated Carmichael for his insensitivity to Jamella and Jamal, even calling him immature and irresponsible to his face, but he laughed at her and stated he had been called worse names.

Then, after Jamella died, Charlene took Jamal

under her wing. She tried to talk to him, influence him in a positive way, but the streets pulled him like a magnet. *If hustling is hereditary, then Jamal is definitely his father's son.*

Her attention focused back to the television screen where Eddie Murphy graced the stage wearing a red leather outfit, reminding her again of Carmichael. She started laughing at Eddie Murphy's fake Jamaican accent, and instantly forgot about Jamella, Jamal, and Carmichael. When her phone rang, she glanced at the clock and noticed it was well past 10:00 p.m. *Maybe it's that fool calling me back.* "Hello," Charlene answered.

"Ms. Smith?" a polite but formal female voice asked. "Ms. Charlene Smith?"

"Yes? Is this a bill collector? I know that you got a whole lot of damn—"

"No, no, ma'am." The woman chuckled. "My name is Ms. Blake. I'm a nurse at Detroit General Hospital. Are you related to Mr. Carmichael Winters?"

"Yes." Charlene's heart beat faster. "Is he all right?"

"Ms. Smith, Mr. Winters has been involved in a serious car accident."

"Oh my God!"

"He is in a coma. We need to make some medical decisions, but we would like to notify family, especially the next of kin, regarding these sensitive matters."

"I understand. Oh my God, when did this happen?"

"Mr. Winters has been hospitalized for approximately one week."

"You know, he has children, a son that I keep in

contact with . . . but he won't be interested. My God, I have to see him. Who can I talk to?"

"Dr. Fletcher is the primary doctor. I can leave a note on his chart. When do you expect to come up here?"

"Tomorrow, about noon. Is that okay?"

"Tomorrow is fine, Ms. Smith. I apologize for disturbing you at this hour, but—"

"No, no, it wasn't a problem at all. Thank you for contacting me," Charlene said before hanging up the phone.

She glanced back at the television, but Eddie Murphy was no longer funny.

Chapter Ten

Jamal put the word on the streets that an emergency meeting was taking place in a couple of hours. A game plan had to be devised because the Chicago Police Department was arresting the Hustlers' upper-level generals, commanders, and everyone else that they could pin something on since the shooting incident involving a six-year-old girl. The shooting flooded the news media, making Englewood the focus of not only local, but national attention. The police learned that a Hustler was responsible for the random shooting, so they were concentrating on them.

Jamal was alarmed that his usual contacts did not inform him of the shakedown.

There was a drought on the street, and Jamal feared that other gangs would use this opportunity to move in on his territory. He kept his gun hidden comfortably in his front trouser, and a smaller pistol taped around his ankle, under his pant cuff.

With every coded knock at the door, Jamal followed the same routine—first signaling for the lights to be turned off, then he would open the door slowly. Only the light from a nearby lamppost illuminated the visitor in the doorway of the garage that served as the meeting place for the Hustlers. Each person was searched before entering.

"Yo, J, is this really necessary?" Darren asked as he was being patted down.

"Where is the boy?" Jamal flopped in a recliner situated in the middle of the garage.

"Dookey's at his aunt's house. Ronnie is keeping watch. Everything's cool. I didn't think you wanted me to bring him here."

"Nah, you did right," he said. "You got my shit?"

"Yeah." Darren tossed a bag to Jamal.

He tore open the bag of flaming hot potato chips with his teeth.

"Dawg, I got two more bags," Darren joked.

A wave of laughter spilled through the garage, easing the tension.

But Jamal did not laugh. "Look, muthafuckas, the po-pos are on our fuckin' asses and messin' up our fuckin' operation. We need to change players, put the shorties out on the streets for the simple shit. We gave Dookey too much responsibility, and look at the shit he made for us. Man, our muthafuckin' pockets are hurtin'." He turned his pants pocket inside out. "We're getting heat from all sides . . . and . . . we not getting our warnings so we can be prepared." He scratched his head. "I have to check that shit out. They took my money. Anyway, shit been real crazy since Dookey shot that girl. Damn, we have to do something. Darren, I want you to take care of the kid."

"J, what you saying? I know you don't mean— Dookey's my muthafuckin' nephew."

"He's a fuckin' liability."

David placed the nicely cut irises on the fresh gravesite. He bent down towards the tombstone— TYRELL PORTER, A SON, A BROTHER, A MAN 1974- 1998. Tears welled in his eyes. *Damn, bro', I miss you so much.* He retrieved a cigarette from his back pocket and lit it. He looked up at the sky and exhaled. *Where are you, man? Up there . . . or down there, causing ruckus? Life is something. When you're young, you believe that you will live forever. You think the whole muthafuckin' world is in your hands, but as you get good and grown, dreams start dying, shit happens, and you hate the path that your life has taken. You tell yourself this is not how I planned for this shit to work out. Remember, bro, when we were younger, you were the smart one, the disciplined and obedient one. I was the wild, crazy child that Momma worried about. She used to whip my ass constantly for being a troublemaker. Oh, did I get my ass whipped, but not you, baby boy. Momma said that she knew you would go to college and major in law or become a doctor. She said that she just prayed that I'd finish high school—ain't that some bullshit. We talked about making money, and I never thought that you would.*

David puffed on his cigarette. *A twist of fate. But*

you loved Momma, and she never stopped loving you. Money is a cruel motivator. You all together; she's back with her baby boy. David forced a chuckle. *Happy birthday, brother. I wish I had some liquor to pour out for ya. Happy Birthday.*

Chapter Eleven

Reese sat on the bed in her motel room and took in her surroundings. The walls were painted a faded yellow. *A color of sickness and deterioration.* Chipped paint particles from the ceiling covered the floor, telling her it hadn't been vacuumed in weeks. Reese sighed. *At least the sheets are clean, and I'm not in Englewood.*

She wasn't strong enough to stay there.

Reese rocked back and forth, trying to calm her nerves and ease her yearning for more cocaine. *One year clean*, she thought to herself. She'd taken pride in announcing to anyone who would listen that she had kicked that habit while others returned to the gutter, back on smack or coke. Now she was dirty again, powerless to the white powdery substance.

Tears of shame ran down her face. *Relapse is part of recovery*, a voice outside her whispered, but that didn't help the disgust that crawled through her. Why had she agreed to use when Tracey tempted her? If anything, she should have stood up to her sister, shown her that the drug no longer had the power it once had. Proved to her that it was possible to break the addiction.

Reese disrobed the clothing she'd worn for two days straight and stepped into the shower. Closing her eyes to the jet spray of warm water washing down on her, she cried despairingly. *Why, God? Why me? Damn!*

She reached for the faucet and turned the water hotter. Then, grabbing a face towel from a nearby bracket, she began to scrub her body in hateful strokes, drawing blood to the surface. She did not flinch when the hot water began to scald her already tender flesh. *A well-deserved punishment*, she thought.

You're a muthafuckin' junkie. Accept your fate.

Reese clutched her head to quiet the voices. "I'm not a junkie, I'm not a junkie, I'm not a junkie," she screamed out, but she had little faith in her words.

Get a little more. You know that you enjoyed it. It wasn't that bad; it was good. Get a little more.

"Shut up," she yelled. "Leave me alone. LEAVE ME ALONE!" She sat nude on the bed, her wet hair dripping down her breasts. She took a long drag on her cigarette, telling herself that the nicotine would soothe her anxieties, but she needed something more, and quick. She snatched her cell phone and called her counselor back in Detroit.

"Hello?" the counselor answered.

"Darla?" Reese asked, her voice trembling.

"Reese, is that you?"

Reese continued to cry through the phone. "Darla, I . . . I . . ."

"You relapsed. You hit the pipe again."

"I'm so sorry. I thought that I could, but I wasn't strong. And Tracey—"

"Chile, slow down. You said *Tracey*. You found her?"

"Yes, I did, and she is worse than they stated. I tried to talk to her, apologize for leaving, but she hates me—"

"Where are you now, Reese?"

"I'm at a motel on Stony Island Avenue."

"A motel? Look, I have a close friend who is an addiction counselor that might be able to help you. You need to get in a detox program—now. Are you feeling the urgency to get some more dope?"

Reese continued to cry through the phone.

"I'm going to call her now. Her name is Crystal Jamieson, and she is good people. I'm going to see if she can get you into their program. Reese, please do not go anywhere until help comes, okay?

"Darla, what about my sister?"

"What have I always told you?" Darla said sternly.

"I can not help anyone else until I help myself."

"Exactly. I will call you back in ten minutes."

Crystal received the urgent phone call from her friend Darla, and agreed to help without hesitation. She knew exactly where the Stony Island Motel was located, for reasons she wanted to forget. Her Bible resting comfortably on the passenger seat of her aged but reliable Toyota Camry—Her decision to turn her life over to the Lord was her best shield of protection—she wasn't afraid of relapsing. She had enjoyed several years of sobriety.

Crystal drove southbound on Jeffrey Boulevard toward 87th Street. She went over in her mind the details that Darla shared with her about Reese, and how important it was that she return to Chicago to find and help her sister.

Crystal flashed back to the days when she lived on the streets. *God help her soul*, Crystal prayed. *She needs you, sweet Jesus.*

Crystal entered the Stony Island Motel parking lot, which was congested with cars. She feared for her personal safety. "I rebuke the devil," she proclaimed out loud. She quickly turned her engine off, grabbed her Bible, and exited her automobile. She ignored the snickers and funny remarks from the patrons loitering in the parking lot and walked confidently to Room 123.

Reese peeped from behind the curtains. "Are you Crystal, Darla's friend?"

Crystal nodded yes and flashed her employee identification card to the window.

Reese unlocked the door and allowed her to come in. "Thank you for coming," Reese said nervously.

Crystal walked in the room cautiously, looking around for anything unusual. She walked to the bathroom and glanced in, pulling the shower curtain to the side. She exhaled in relief, certain she and Reese were the only ones in the room.

"No one else is here," Reese affirmed, reading Crystal's behavior.

"God bless . . ." Crystal stopped midstream to

watch Reese fidget with her cigarette. "So you said you been clean for one year?"

"Yeah. Is that what Darla shared with you? I hope that she didn't tell you every little detail of my life. I hope that confidentiality is still the law."

Crystal was taken aback by Reese's attitude. "Look, she told me what she needed to tell me. I agreed to help her help you, okay. If you don't want to go, I can leave. We can simply call her now and—"

"No, no. Thank you. I didn't mean to be rude. I'm just angry at myself for being in this mess. I thought that I was stronger than this, and look how I fucked up."

Crystal walked to Reese and draped her arm around her shoulder.

Reese allowed herself to cry on Crystal's shoulder.

"You know you're stronger than the drugs. You reached out and called for help. That's proof in itself that you're stronger than you give yourself credit for."

"I don't feel strong; I feel weak and helpless. I mean, I'm trying to help my sister, and yet I can't get a grip on my own addiction."

"That's the beauty of the drug. It strips away at your self-confidence, turns you into something ugly. Believe me, I know. I been down that road several times, but you can't give up. The devil cannot be victorious, and you cannot help anyone until you help yourself."

"I want my sister to believe what Darla finally got into me. She's so much better than whorin' and druggin' out on those streets. And if she don't stop, I fear—"

Crystal glanced down at her watch. "Look, sweetie, we have to go. They're expecting us at the program."

When Reese began gathering her personal belongings, a news bulletin flashed on the television propped in the corner of the motel room. The reporter was standing in front of Ole Manny Liquor Store. Reese grabbed the remote control to raise the volume.

"Another female has been brutally raped in the Englewood area. This is the second rape within four days. This second victim, identified as Tracey Clark, remains in critical condition at John Stronger Hospital."

Reese fainted to the floor.

Mourners waved paper and plastic fans, trying to comfort themselves in the smoldering heat of Old Zion Church, situated in the heart of Englewood. Desperate cries reverberated from every corner of the church, each wail enticing another of louder proportion.

"Oh God, he's just a child," an overwhelmed griever shouted. She staggered to the closed casket.

The small, pearlized white casket, trimmed with gold accessories and draped with flowers and cards of condolences, sat high at the head of the aisle in the small frame church, overflowing with family members, friends, and neighbors of young Anthony Paxton, also known as "Dookey."

Anthony's classmates from Hixton Elementary School lined up somberly, wearing matching red T-shirts that read in bold block letters: THE VIOLENCE MUST STOP. NO MORE VICTIMS. Each classmate walked past the miniature casket and wrote a personal inscription on the giant card positioned directly in front of the coffin.

Reverend Baldwin stood solemnly to the left of the pulpit and looked despairingly out at the congregation. Presiding over funerals was an important function of his ministering. And he could always reach for the right words of comfort to help the grieving, especially when the deceased died of natural causes. But young Anthony had his whole life in front of him, and his words would bring small comfort to Anthony's mother, or the community.

As the Reverend looked out, he wished his church would overflow with all these people every Sunday, but his pews remained relatively empty unless, of course, it was a funeral. Gang violence brought too many victims to him. Reverend Baldwin steadied his eyes down on the despondent mother, so young herself, who sat stone-faced in the front row. Her eyes, frozen to the coffin in front of her, never wandered off.

Lines of people walked to her to offer sympathy and support, but she could only mumble a robotic, "Thank you. Thank you." Her eleven-year-old son was gone.

Next to the mother sat a young man the reverend had only a seen a few times in the community, usually one in a large group of neighborhood punks. *Jarod? Derek? No, Darren.* His face, too, had a hard look, nearly emotionless . . . except the reverend saw a deeper meaning behind the cold, unmoving eyes—anger.

Chapter Twelve

"She's fuckin' MIA, I told you. I told you we couldn't trust her. Once an addict, always an addict, but you assholes wouldn't listen. Because of her the whole muthafucka operation is blown. We need to get another angle." The detective stormed out of the office on a rant. She secretly enjoyed being proven right in front of this men's club and enjoyed rubbing it in more.

"Shut the fuck up, Paula," Joe said. "I don't fucking want to hear your sorry 'I told you so,' okay? Maybe you're right, maybe not. Happy? Eat a damn cookie."

"Fuck you, Joe," the female detective replied.

"Maybe that's what the fuck's wrong with you, Paula. Having a dry spell?"

"Will the both of you shut up. You're both ranting like bitches. Now I need your attention." Sergeant Smith banged on the desk. "When is the last time anyone heard from her?"

"It's been two days, and she hasn't given us any information that we can use against Jamal. She fuckin' using again. I know it."

"Sarge, we need more time. She's only been here a short time. I believe she can pull this off and we can bring the Hustlers down, and with shit that's going to stick, not circumstantial bullshit. She can get close to Jamal, but it takes time to earn trust," Joe explained.

"Sarge, I say we round them up in a bogus sting operation by inviting them to a concert. We can put some famous rappers on the letter, lure them to the spot, and arrest their asses. We already got shit on Darren, Jimmy, Derrick, Timothy, and we certainly can get one of 'em to drop Jamal," Paula said.

"What ya got on those punks?" Joe asked. "A case of trafficking? Possession? What ya got?"

"Enough to bring their asses in and charged," Paula hurled back. "A few years off the streets is better than investing in some dumb broad—an addict, mind you—waiting for I don't know how long to get more what? He has outstanding parking tickets? Come on, Joe, get your head outta your ass."

"Joe, I'm with Paula. If she's using, she has already compromised the operation. I don't believe that she can be trusted. Is she using again, Joe?" the sergeant asked.

"No," Joe lied.

"Don't fuckin' lie, Joe. You said you followed her to that damn rat-infested hole on Loomis, where all the junkies live."

"She went there because that's where her sister lives, if you must know."

"And? She could be working both sides against

the middle. She hasn't kept in contact with us, and that was a part of the program."

"She's right, Joe," the sergeant affirmed.

"Look," Joe explained, "I know that, but I told her to loosen up on the contact. She needs time to get in and form a relationship with Jamal again."

"She still could find time to keep us informed. Sarge, I say abandon the junkie and we find another way in."

"Why are you so quick to call her names?"

"I call them like I see them."

"I believe you're fuckin' jealous of her. Yeah, that must be it. She is desirable, while you look like a dude."

"Y'all need to slow down with this shit. We're on the same team, okay. Don't forget that." Sergeant Smith looked directly at Paula, then back at Joe. "Y'all bicker like you're married."

"Shit! Not to her. Times will never get that desperate."

"Suck my dick."

"Yeah, I knew you had one."

The sergeant shook his head. "We're changing course. We're going to do another sweep in the next couple of days. Paula, put the info you got on my desk. I will review it first thing in the morning." The sergeant walked out of the room, still shaking his head.

"Sarge, I think that's a bad idea. We have already conducted sweeps in Englewood. Another one and they will definitely get more suspicious. I think we should chill a little while longer so that—"

The sergeant turned. "Joe, I'm afraid I can't do

that. I'm getting pressure from the lieutenant, the mayor, and the public to do something. With everything going on in Englewood, they already think the police don't care and are not doing their job. We need to do something, Joe. I'm afraid we don't have the time to chill."

"So you're giving in to political pressure," Joe said sarcastically. "I thought you were stronger than that."

"I don't give a fuck what you think." The sergeant pointed his finger in Joe's face. "I'm the one in charge. Don't forget that. As far as I'm concerned, your way, usin' that road, has proven to be a waste of time and a fuckin' headache. Paula, I'm expecting that info on my desk nine A.M. sharp."

"Nine a.m. sharp. Roger that."

Joe caught her smirk as she exited the room.

Joe jumped into his unmarked Buick and sped out of the parking lot. He wasn't ready to give up Reese, but he knew his margin of time was small. Very small. He needed to get Reese closer to Jamal, so the operation would not be compromised. His mind was a blank. Joe refused to admit in front of Paula and the sergeant that he'd followed Reese up to her sister's room and found her on the floor. She had relapsed. He helped get her back to the motel outside of Englewood, the one he had arranged for her, thinking it would be safe. She woke up long enough to apologize for her actions, but he understood junkies. He knew all too well the lies they told—mostly to themselves. The window to get action on Jamal was closing, and Reese would be on the outside looking in. Joe needed her to act fast, demonstrate her loyalty to Jamal, get him on her side, but how?

He drove into the Stony Island Motel parking lot and jogged to Reese's door. Perhaps she had an idea. He was willing to listen to almost anything at this point. He knocked forcefully for several minutes. When no one answered, he leaned in close to the window and put his ear against the glass, hoping to hear movement inside, but the room appeared quiet.

He knocked again, this time banging. Still no answer. *Maybe she went to get something to eat.* He looked beyond the parking lot to the few eating establishments lining the area. *I told her not to go anywhere.* He walked across the motel parking lot to the lobby.

"Hey," Joe said to the male clerk behind the desk.

The male clerk batted his eyes seductively at Joe. "Yes?"

"I was wondering if you could tell me if my friend in Room 123 checked out."

"Now, you know I'm not allowed to disclose that information, sir," the clerk replied flirtatiously.

"Look, this is important." Joe flashed his badge. "I need to know."

"Okay, okay, you don't have to get your panties all bunched up."

"What didja say?"

"Your friend in Room 123 did check out. Pretty girl, shoulder-length hair, about my complexion."

"Yeah, that's her."

"She threw the keys on the counter and left. She looked upset, like she'd been crying. You didn't make her cry now, did you, honey?"

"You know—"

"Just teasing, just teasing. I wanted to see you smile."

Frustrated, Joe turned to leave the office.

"Oh, did I mention she was with an older lady toting a Bible? Maybe they went to Bible study."

"Maybe," Joe replied as he exited the door.

Chapter Thirteen

Charlene flipped through pages of *Essence* magazine as she waited for Dr. Fletcher to return
from lunch. She glanced down at her watch—2:00
P.M. She was told that the doctor was due back in an
hour. That was at noon. Charlene tiptoed down the
hallway towards the intensive care unit, where
Carmichael, still unconscious, was hooked up to a
respirator to assist with his breathing, a maze of
tubes running from his arms, nose, and chest to the
machinery at the head of his bed.

The nurse was brief with Charlene, not releasing
any additional information beyond the obvious.
"You have to follow up with Dr. Fletcher, regarding
any medical information."

Charlene had a laundry list of questions. She
glanced at her watch again, and paced, finally returning to the waiting area to flip through the magazines a second time until the doctor returned.

Tired of re-reading the same magazines, Charlene decided to pass the time by cleaning out her purse. She dumped the contents on the seat next to her and was astonished by the number of receipts and papers stuffed in her small purse. She thumbed through the receipts—one from Walgreens, when she'd purchased toilet tissues on sale, a receipt from Kentucky Fried Chicken, another from Auto Zone, and another from the Pleasure Chest.

She smiled at that two-month-old receipt for sex toys. They'd been pretty expensive, but well worth it. She laughed at herself.

As she gathered up all the receipts for the trash, she spotted a phone number, lightly written in pencil, on the back of the Pleasure Chest receipt—Jamal's cell phone number. Charlene quickly grabbed her cell phone and dialed the number. It went straight to his voicemail.

"Damn." She searched her phone directory and noticed that she had another number for Jamal. She quickly dialed the second number.

"Holla," Jamal answered.

"Jamal, baby, this is Charlene. How are you?"

"Hey, Charlene. I'm chillin'. What's happenin'?"

"Baby, I got some bad news to tell you."

"What? Are you okay? What's wrong?"

"Carmichael, your daddy was involved in a car accident, sugar. He's in intensive care at Detroit General Hospital. He's in a coma."

"What's the bad news? You know I don't give a fuck about that dude."

"Jamal!"

"Sorry, Charlene, but you know how I feel about him."

"I know, baby, but I think you should come up

here. I'm waiting for the doctor now, trying to get word on his condition."

"I'm not coming up there."

"Jamal, I need for you to come," Charlene lied. "On the way up here, my car ran into problems. You know I got that old car, and . . . please, Jamal, I don't ask you for much. Have I asked you for anything?"

"How much you need? I can wire you whatever you need. You know I got your back."

Charlene searched for another excuse. "Baby, I was hoping that you would drive your truck. I have a few things . . . and your father has things I'm bringing home. Detroit is only four hours away. Please . . ."

"Aunt Charlene, I will come only to help you bring your sh—stuff back." Jamal remembered not to curse in front of Charlene. "I'm not going to see him. I don't care if he lives or dies. I can come some-time tomorrow." He thought it might be a good time to get out of town.

"Thank you, sugar. Aunt Charlene appreciates it. You know that." She kissed the receiver.

Chapter Fourteen

David lay sprawled across his futon, watching DVD's, one after the other. He'd been living on edge for the last few days, pacing the floor, even polishing his gun, not knowing what else to do with his time but wait for Tracey to call. It angered him that she left him hanging out, with no way to get in touch with her. He continually re-evaluated the consequences of his pursuit to hunt down Jamal and Reese. One thing for sure, it cost him quite a bit of his savings. David expected that, but he had nothing to show for it. He didn't expect to spend day after day in one room.

He looked at his small collection of guns that he had purchased. *This shit needs to be over.* He wondered how he could scheme money out of Jamal and kill him at the same time. *Shit.* Too many damn questions, not enough answers.

He reached over to his nightstand to retrieve his

cell phone and dialed a friend whose voice he hadn't heard in months.

"Hello," she answered.

"Hey, Vanessa," David said, warmed to hear her familiar voice.

"David? Wow! It's been a while since I heard from you. How are you doing?"

"All right, I guess. How are you?"

"I'm great. No complaints. You know me, busy as ever. I just finished my appraisal classes, and I'll take the state exam in a couple of months. My bookstore is expanding, and I'm so excited. I'm in Chicago for—"

"You're in Chicago?" David sat up on his bed.

"Yes, I'm in Chicago. Why are you so excited?"

"Where are you staying?"

"David?"

"Vanessa, I'm in Chicago too. I'm leasing out an apartment for . . . a temporary assignment. I'm in Hyde Park. Where are you? How long will you be staying?"

"I'm at the Hyatt, across from the Lake. The address is"—She reached in the drawer to retrieve the hotel directory—"The address is 4949 South Lake Shore Drive. You know where that's at?"

David tried to control his enthusiasm. "Vanessa, you're in walking distance of my apartment."

"Are you living in Chicago now?"

"Let's have dinner, my treat, and I will answer all of your questions."

"You don't have to ask me twice. Where?"

"Your hotel has a fabulous restaurant. How about 7:30?"

"It's 6:55 now."

"A brother's hungry!" David pulled a fresh crisp shirt and matching trousers from his closet.

"Cool, 7:30. See you then, David!"

David jumped in and out of the shower in less than five minutes. He quickly dressed in his casual attire, surprised at how little it took to bring him out of his dark mood. He looked forward to an evening of good food and good conversation, relieved that he could put thoughts of Tracey, Reese, Jamal, and his brother's death to sleep for a night.

Grabbing his jacket, he headed out into the Chicago spring air, glad he'd decided to walk. David walked down 47th Street past Bally Total Fitness Gym, past Hyde Park Co-op, past Coop's Records, until he descended under the V-docks. He found himself humming Brian McKnight's "Anytime."

David crossed the service ramp that led to Lake Shore Drive, and cut across the hotel's parking lot. He glanced down at his watch—7:25. *Perfect timing*. He spotted Vanessa immediately, sitting at the bar, drinking a glass of wine.

"Hello, stranger." He reached out to give her an embrace and a friendly kiss on her cheek.

"Hello to you, too, Mr. I'm So Busy."

"Okay, I deserve that."

"Nah, I'm just teasing," she said, tapping David playfully on his arm.

"Girl, it's just so good to see you. It's been—"

"What have you been doing with yourself, Mr. Davenport? We sort of drifted apart, or, shall I say, you stopped calling. I know you mentioned something about your job, but I never bought that excuse."

"It wasn't an excuse; it *was* my damn job—Hey, bartender, I'll have a White Russian." He turned back to Vanessa. "Is this going to be a night of interrogation?"

"No, no, we already had that conversation. I forget we saw each other several times after our 'unofficial' breakup." She laughed. "But it's been about—"

"Two years."

"Yeah, two years. You miss me, David?" She surprised him by moving her big toe underneath his pant cuff.

"Yes, I missed you, Ms. Vanessa. We always had a good time together."

"Let's make a toast." Vanessa lifted her glass in the air, and David followed.

"What are we toasting to?"

"Good times. We're toasting to having damn good times. Life is too short for the rest of this bullshit."

"I agree, life is too damn short." David smiled, his glass raised to hers. He knew Vanessa was becoming intoxicated from the wine.

The two sat in the lounge for over three hours drinking and talking and drinking some more.

When they agreed to go to the restaurant, the host informed them that the restaurant had closed thirty minutes earlier. Vanessa burst out laughing.

David gently grabbed her arms and led her back into the lounge.

"I know you think I'm drunk, but I'm well aware of my actions."

"That's good to know. I don't want you passing out on me. I'm having too much fun." He looked up at the television positioned in the corner of the room to catch the basketball highlights.

"Still a basketball junkie?"

"All day long."

The volume was barely above a whisper, so David asked the bartender to increase the sound so he could hear the commentaries of the sports announcer.

"Bored, Mr. Davenport?" Vanessa walked behind David as he stood listening to the sports newsman. She rubbed his ass.

He turned around, surprised. "Not the least," he said into her ear.

Vanessa began a slow and deliberate gyration, her hips slowly grinding his.

"The bartender is ready for us to leave," he murmured. "He's putting up the chairs and wiping off the table. Soon he is going to cut off the television."

"We can finish this in my room," she whispered, taking David's hand in hers. "Let's go."

David pulled back. "Wait just a sec. Let me catch the ending of the sports highlights."

"Is it that serious?" Vanessa folded her arms across her chest in protest.

"Nah, hell nah." He kissed her briefly on the lips. "But it's back on now." He laughed. "Thirty seconds, okay, and I'm yours for the rest of the night."

"Okay, thirty seconds—one, two, three . . ."

Ignoring Vanessa, David inched back to the television, but the sports commentary did not resume. *Damn, I missed it.* Instead, they were summarizing the highlights of the daily news, including the unsolved rapes.

A photo of Tracey Clark appeared on the screen, freezing David.

. . . Tracey Clark, the latest victim and most seriously injured, indicates that the rapist is increasing his violence against women. Ms. Clark remains in critical condition . . .

Vanessa whined, "David, baby, come on . . . you promised."

Reese convinced Crystal to take her to John Stronger Hospital so she could visit with her sister. "Besides, Crystal, I'm her only relative. They may need me to sign papers. They're always looking for the next of kin, or closest relative, ya know, to give the go-ahead to treat the patient."

Crystal was reluctant, believing the visit could cause more harm than good.

Crystal prayed quietly as she drove onto the Eisenhower Expressway towards John Stronger Hospital. *Jesus, my Savior, touch this girl's heart so that she may endure the sight of her sister. Jesus, may Your healing blood bring her back from the brink of death. Jesus, You're a merciful God. Heal Lord, Heal with power of Your love. Amen.*

"Are you sure you want to see your sister, now?" Crystal asked. "Maybe you can call the hospital instead."

"Stop." Reese, clearly irritated by Crystal's question, suddenly wanted the woman to go away. "Your question, Crystal, tells me you only know about addiction. You don't understand, obviously, that if I jumped into rehab and my sister died, I would never want to get clean again. You can leave if you want, but I'm going to my sister. She needs me. I need to be needed."

Crystal fought back tears as she vividly remembered receiving the devastating news that her beloved brother, Samuel Jamieson, and his wife died in a horrible car accident.

"No, you're right. I wouldn't call; I would be at the hospital in a heartbeat," she said. *I would now.*

Years ago, when Crystal received news that her brother and sister-in-law were in an automobile accident, and that they were transported to Loyola Hospital in Maywood, she remembered telling the hospital nurse, "They're in good hands. I'll check on them in the morning." Samuel and his wife died later that night. Crystal was busy smoking crack with her friends, having too good a time to take the long ride from the South Side to the western suburbs. She never got to say good-bye.

"Go see about your sister, chile."

"Sorry, visiting hours are over," the security guard announced to the two women panting hard from the run from the parking lot to the hospital entrance.

"Look," Reese pleaded, "I just found out about my sister. I saw it on TV. Please . . . can I have her information? Call up to the station. They'll let me up; I guarantee you. I'm her only next of kin."

It took the guard only minutes to confirm that Reese, indeed, should be allowed to go up to ICU. "Go on up. Intensive care is on the seventh floor." He pointed at Crystal. "Is that lady with you?"

"Yes, she's Tracey's sister too," Reese lied.

He handed Reese two guest passes, but not before he reached out and touched her hand. "She is going to be fine."

His simple kindness brought tears to Reese's eyes. "Thank you," she said. "Thank you very much!"

Crystal and Reese rode the elevator up to the seventh floor in silence.

"The Lord is good," Crystal said, trying to offer words of encouragement.

"Then why would the Lord allow this to happen to my sister, if He is so damn good?"

"Chile, my God is a healing God. But you got to believe and pray for your sister."

Reese walked out without commenting, and Crystal followed her down the long corridor that led to the intensive care unit.

"Tracey, I'm coming," Reese mumbled to herself. "I'm coming. You're going to get better. I'm going to cut the muthafucka that did this to you, and then I'm going to fuck Jamal up for getting you hooked on this shit."

"Pardon me? Were you talkin' to me?"

Reese turned sharply on Crystal. "I said I'm gonna kill all the muthafuckas that did this to me and mine."

Crystal drew back and watched Reese march with determination down the hall. She waited several feet back against the wall as Reese approached the nursing station to inquire about her sister.

A nurse walked around the station, a warm smile on her face, but Crystal couldn't mistake the seriousness in her eyes.

The two began a slow walk in her direction,

heads down. Crystal wondered if she should involve herself, but as they passed, Reese never looked up.

The nurse asked, "Are you Tracey's only next of kin?"

Reese nodded.

David followed Vanessa back to her room, Tracey's name ringing in his thoughts. It became clear why she'd not made contact. He silently apologized for accusing her of being trifling. He thought about abruptly ending the night, walking Vanessa safely to her room, and returning to the sanctuary of his apartment to digest the news.

But Vanessa had other plans. Giggling, she pulled David along by his arm until they got to her door. She stepped forward to kiss him with an intensity that left nothing to the imagination. She started to unbutton his shirt.

"Vanessa, can we get in the room?"

She smiled and handed him her key. As the door closed, Vanessa pressed into him, clawing at his shirt and pants until they were abandoned near the bathroom entrance. She stripped off her clothes in haste and sat on top of the desk in a butterfly position.

David, walking towards her, tripped over her purse and hit his head on the side of the desk. "Damn!" He sat on the edge of the bed and rubbed his abrasion.

Vanessa got off the desk and stroked the injured area with her nipple.

He grabbed her hungrily by the waist and threw her onto the bed. The constant ache of his brother's death, the news of Tracey's rape, and the throbbing pain of his head injury were all released through his desperate thrusting on Vanessa, but she felt no pain or sorrow and rode the waves of David's body, matching his vigor and intensity, until both their bodies collapsed from exertion and exhilaration.

Chapter Fifteen

Darren draped the hood of his sweatshirt over his head and leaned against the gray stone building. His heart was palpitating, and his hands were sweaty. He looked up and down the street several times, hoping that no one followed him, and more importantly that nobody recognized him. The empty streets eased his tension, and the gun nestled in his sweatshirt pocket for easy access gave him the confidence to make his next move.

He ran across the street to a faded brown-framed, three-story building. The sound of male chatter greeted him on his ascension to the top of the porch. A motion detector that generated the overhead lights acknowledged his presence before he could ring the doorbell.

"What cha want?" A man stood behind Darren at the base of the stairs and pointed an automatic rifle.

Darren was so shaken he did not hear the man's footsteps coming behind him. "I want to see Guy."

"Guy want to see you? Come here." The man motioned for Darren to walk down the steps.

He obliged, but kept his focus on the young man, and the rifle pointed directly at his chest. He walked down the stairs slowly, his hands elevated. He knew the routine all too well.

The man patted him down.

"I'm strapped. You know that no one can walk these streets without being protected."

The man removed the gun from Darren's sweatshirt. "What cha wanna see Guy about? He ain't down with uninvited guests."

"Look, I got some news for him that will be, let's say, profitable."

"Yeah, yeah. I heard that shit before . . . wastin' my muthafuckin' time."

"Look, I know who killed one of your gang members," Darren said confidently. "And I got some info that will be valuable to Guy. Now, I know you don't want to have him bust a cap in yo' ass if he finds out that I was here and you—"

"Come on, muthafucka." The man escorted Darren in the house. "This shit better be good, or I'ma blast your ass myself."

"I wouldn't fuckin' be here if it wasn't."

Darren was blindfolded before entering the building complex. He was led by muscular hands up a set of stairs, down a long corridor, up another set of stairs, and then down a few flights of stairs.

When the blindfold was removed, he found himself in an ordinary room with a large-screen television, a pool table positioned against the wall, and a coffee table that served as a card table. Darren immediately recognized Guy as one of the dudes playing bid whist.

As he shuffled the cards, Guy looked up briefly at Darren. "Who this muthafucka?"

"He said that he wanted to talk you."

"And I don't want to talk to him."

"I need to talk to you, Guy, alone." Darren pushed his hood down, exposing his identity.

Immediately recognizing Darren from the Hustlers, Guy jumped up from the table and grabbed his gun. "You let this fool in?"

"Yeah. What's the problem? He's been searched."

"Look, Guy, I came here to give you some info that will fatten your muthafuckin' pocket."

"Either you a dumb, stupid-ass muthafucka for comin' here, or, dawg, yo' ass got something worth listening to."

"Can I?" Darren looked at a chair.

"Nah, your ass can't sit down. Stand the fuck up. Yo' ass ain't welcome here. This is not a damn Holiday Inn. Get to the point."

Darren looked around the room and counted eight men.

"They not leavin'," Guy said, reading Darren's thoughts.

"I need to talk to you alone." Darren walked up closer to Guy and whispered, "I know who killed Shaun. Hear me out."

Finally Guy motioned for the other men to leave, but not before positioning a gun in Darren's face. "Get to talkin', muthafucka, and this shit better be good for interrupting my game and my goddamn time."

"Can I sit down?"

"Hell, nah, your ass still ain't welcome here. I told your retarded ass this place ain't a fuckin' lounge. Get to the point, muthafucka."

"Okay, okay. Jamal killed Shaun with that damn gun yo' boy confiscated from me. Jamal thought the Cobras was responsible for his brother Jun-Jun's death, so he kidnapped Shaun and questioned him. Shaun kept telling him that the Cobras were not responsible, but Jamal shot him in the head anyway."

"And you tellin' me this for what? And why should I believe yo' stupid ass?" Guy retorted, a wash of spit hitting Darren in the face. "Jamal is yo' dawg, you rollin' with his crew, and comin' over here tellin' me this bull. You on some suicidal shit or what?"

"Look, you don't have any reason to believe me, but Jamal killed my young cousin, Dookey, who was trying to imitate his ass. Shot him in the head. He was only eleven."

"And?"

"I'm going to destroy the muthafucka from the inside out."

"Oh really? You're a dead muthafucka, you know that?"

"I don't give a fuck. I know that, and he is going to be a dead muthafucka too."

"What all this shit got to do with me?"

"With Jamal out the way . . . with Jamal out of the picture, you can move in and take over his territory."

Guy smirked as the idea began to take form.

*   *   *

Reese closed her eyes and said a quiet prayer before entering her sister's room. The intensive care unit had a smell that was different than other parts of the hospital. It smelled like blood and ammonia mixed together. Reese looked back and saw that Crystal lingered back by the nursing station, and she was glad. She slowly opened the door to the humming and clicking sounds of the machinery hooked up to Tracey. She walked over to the side of her sister's bed and nearly tripped over the IV bag.

Tears poured down her face. "What has that monster done to you?"

Reese turned to the window and looked out into the darkness. She looked back at her sister and cried out in rage.

A concerned nurse scurried into the room. "Is everything okay in here?"

"No, everything is not all right. Look at my sister . . . look at her."

The nurse walked over to Reese and held her. "She's not in any pain," the nurse said softly. "We're doing all we can. She's getting good care. She will pull through this. We're all praying for her."

"I'm tired of hearing that. Why would God do this to my sister? I'm praying and praying, but look at her. God is not hearing my prayers."

Crystal walked through the door. "Don't do that. You have to keep your faith. You must not waver. You have to remain strong and know that God has a plan."

"Yeah, God's plan was for my sister to get stabbed and raped."

The nurse walked past Crystal and patted her gently on the shoulders. She looked back at Reese sympathetically. "Ring the bell if you need anything. And she's right—you must keep the faith. You must continue to believe. If you want to talk to someone like a priest or social worker, I can—"

Reese waved her away.

"Amen," Crystal said.

Reese pulled up a chair closer to Tracey's bed and began to rub her hands and arms. "I'm so sorry, Tracey. If I would have—"

"It's not your fault, Reese, it's not your fault."

"It is. I deserted her. I was all she had, but I deserted her. Because I listened to him." Her voice gradually changed to anger. "That bastard!"

"Who?"

"Nothing, nothing." Reese started to pace the hospital room.

"Look, I know what you goin' through. It's hard when you think you're trying to do the right thing and stuff like this happens, throwing you off your center."

"What? This ain't no shit just happenin'. My damn sister is in a damn coma because she was raped by some sick-ass muthafucka. I deserted her, and the only person that she thought she had . . . well, his ass ain't around."

"Look, this anger that's coming over you won't help your sister."

Reese stopped pacing momentarily to look at Crystal. "You're right," she lied. "I need to calm down. Look, I'm going to the nurse's station to ask her a question. I'll be right back."

"Okay." Crystal sat down in the chair next to Tracey's bed and opened her Bible to read an inspirational quote.

Reese walked out of the hospital room, past the nursing station. The nurse on the phone looked up and smiled at her as she walked past. Reese did not acknowledge her greeting and kept walking until she got on the elevator. She stepped out of the hospital into a downpour of rain and walked eastbound down Harrison Street for a couple of blocks. She had to clear her head.

Realizing she had no place to go, she entered a greasy spoon to get dry and use the pay phone.

"Where the fuck you been?" he screamed through the phone. "I've been trying like hell to get in contact with you. You don't return calls."

"Joe, can you come get me?"

"Come get you? Where in the hell are you?"

"I just left John Stronger Hospital. I'm at Harrison Hot Dog Shack."

"I know where it's at. I'm not that far from there. I can be there in about ten minutes. This damn conversation is not over. You have fucked up a lot of shit, and I want an explanation."

"I'll see you when you get here," she said.

Joe arrived in front of Harrison Hot Dog Shack in less than five minutes, fuming with anger. As he walked into the poorly lit establishment, he spotted Reese sitting on a bar stool in the corner, devouring a hot dog. His left hand balled up into a fist as he walked up on her. "Reese, where the hell have you been?"

"Did you know that my sister was brutally raped? She's currently in the hospital fighting for her life."

"No, I didn't know. I'm sorry to hear that, but that doesn't change shit. You fucked up everything. The operation is basically blown because you failed to keep your part and stay in contact. I'm telling you, you really fucked up. I thought I could count on you. Remember our game plan?"

"Yeah, I remember, but I haven't heard anything. Jamal hasn't said shit to me, and I really haven't been around him. He hasn't seen me in five years, and you really thought that he was going to spill everything to me. I don't think so."

"Look," Joe said calmly, "I went through a lot of shit with the cops not to charge you with anything. You agreed to do this, remember? So don't give me bullshit. This whole operation is blown. I simply asked you to maintain contact with me. That is not a hard task. You haven't responded to my calls. I put you up at the Stony Island Motel, and then I learned you checked out with another woman. What the fuck is goin' on with you?"

"I told you I found out about my sister. So I called my counselor, and she called her friend Crystal, who was supposed to take me to a detox center. But I convinced her to take me to the hospital."

"You could have asked me. I could have taken you, found out about your sister's status, or whatever you needed to ease your mind. But you didn't ask me. You called your counselor in Detroit, instead of me right here in Chicago. My partner wants to abandon this whole operation. They don't have faith in your ability to bring Jamal down. They think—"

"I'm too tired to give a fuck what they think . . . or what you think, for that matter." Reese tossed her drinking cup in a nearby trash bin. "I know what I agreed to, but the shit is not working out as planned, okay. I haven't spoken to Jamal since his brother was killed, and he hasn't told me anything worth reporting. And I'm worn out—"

"Okay, okay. When was the last time you saw Jamal?"

"I told you, not since his brother was killed."

"Look, I need for you to get back in contact with him, and try to stay close."

"How can I stay close, if he doesn't want me around?"

"You have to stay close. I don't know. Pretend he is the only one that you know now, or you don't have nowhere else to turn or something. Shit, I want to put a wire on you."

"You want my ass muthafuckin' killed? I'm not wearing a damn wire."

"It's your last option, or your services ain't needed. The operation is a total failure. I'll contact the DA and tell them the operation is over, and they might go ahead and charge you with first-degree murder. It's really their call. That one-year stint in prison is nothing compared to looking at 20 years to life for Tyrell Porter's murder."

"Stop it," Reese yelled. "I'm not going to prison. They can't do that. I didn't murder Tyrell." She bent over and started to cry. "I need help. I need to get in a drug treatment center, Joe. Will you help me?"

Joe ordered a cup of coffee as he pondered Reese's question. "I agree that you need a drug treatment program, but I don't see how that would fit in the scheme of things now. I really don't."

"But I need help. I was totally helpless when Tracey put that pipe to my lips. That craving has entered back into my body."

"Have you used again since then?"

"No, but . . ."

"We will address your drug problem, but we need to stay focused."

Reese saw his frustration, but his lack of concern for her, his determination to use her at the expense of her addiction, frightened her more than another stint in prison. She didn't think she could make it on her own, especially once she entered Jamal's world.

"Look, I need to drop you back off in Engle-wood. You need to find Jamal and stay close to him. Get me information we can run with, anything to sustain the operation. My boss is already looking at other ways to get what we need. I have to convince him now to keep you on. If you don't produce, it's out of my hands; and this shit is down the toilet, and I'll be sure you go with it."

"Joe, is there any way—"

"No, there is no other way. You fucked up. Fix it."

"But my sister, what about my sister?"

"I thought this plan *was* about your sister, since you blame Jamal for getting her strung out, but it looks like you are abandoning her again."

"Fuck you, Joe!"

"You're already doing that, and doing it well. Look, I'm dropping you off around Jamal's crib. You need to find him somehow and report back with something of substance within the next forty-eight hours or—"

"Or what?"

"You know the answer to that question."

Chapter Sixteen

Jamal tossed a change of clothing in his duffle bag and threw it in his SUV. He didn't want to make the four-hour drive to Detroit, but he needed to get out of town for a day or so. He would never say no to Charlene, who was like a second mother to him. He laughed at the news that his father was dying in a Detroit hospital, but there was no laughter when he thought about Tracey. He wanted to go to John Stranger Hospital to check on her condition, but he didn't want to risk running into any police that would be attached to her case.

He put word out on the street that a finder's fee would be paid to the individual who gave him information about the creep responsible for Tracey's rape. If he were still in Chicago, Jamal was confident he would be found and dealt with accordingly.

Too much shit was happening too damn fast, and Jamal felt like he was losing control. Yeah, the trip out of town to Detroit was what he needed. He didn't tell anyone he was leaving. He was becoming increasingly suspicious of everyone, trusting only a selective few, including Reese, with his second cell phone number.

He popped in Kanye's CD and bopped his head to the lyrics of "Slow Jam." He set his cruise control on 65 miles per hour as he entered onto Highway 94, to guard against the temptation of speeding.

As he drove down the dark highway, Jamal wondered whether he would have any money to inherit if Carmichael died. *Nah, that broke muthafucka don't have a penny, and all them damn kids he got.*

He thought about his own son. He adored three-year-old Jabaree, the only positive thing in his life. The thought of Jabaree growing up in the foster care system frightened him. *His poppa is a drug dealer, and his mother a crackhead.* "I got to hurry up and get out of the game," he said out loud.

The idea had crossed his mind several times in the last year. He smiled as he recalled a conversation with his brother, Jun-Jun.

"What ya gonna do, man—work at Mickey D's or KFC?" Jun-Jun would tease.

"Hell nah, muthafucka," Jamal told him. "I would get us some real estate, and maybe start up a recording company. Shit, most of the muthafucka rappers used to sling. Hell, if they can do it, so can we."

Jun-Jun warmed to the idea. He even came up with the name for the company—Street Soldiers Productions—and joked that he would be the first artist to be released on their recording label.

* * *

Darren left Guy's apartment, suddenly second-guessing his arrangement with the Cobras. He stopped to listen for footsteps, and looked over his shoulders for anyone that might be following him. The streets were still.

His first thought was to take his story to the police, but he knew that he would open a Pandora's box, bringing out other murders that would incriminate him before he wrote his first name on the arrest sheet. *Fuck it, fuck it, that muthafucka is dead tonight. I don't care about nothing.*

He removed the gun from his sweatshirt and checked the chamber to ensure that it was filled with bullets. He put the gun back in the pocket of his sweatshirt and kept his right hand attached to the trigger. When he stopped to gauge the traffic before crossing Ashland Boulevard, he saw Reese jump out of a black four-door Buick, very similar to an undercover police car. He watched curiously as the vehicle pulled off.

Reese looked dazed. She started to walk southbound down Ashland.

Darren ran up quietly behind her and put the gun in her back. "We need to talk, Ms. Thang," he whispered into her ear.

Reese looked over her shoulder into Darren's face and released a sigh. "Okay."

Darren stuck the gun deeper into her back and motioned for her to walk. "Who was that you were with?"

"A detective."

"A cop?"

"I went to go see my sister at the hospital. The detectives were there asking me questions. I told them I didn't know anything. Hell, I *don't* know anything. He offered me a ride home, so I took it."

"So why didn't you go home? Why'd you have him drop you off on this corner?"

"Because . . . I don't trust the cops, okay. And I didn't give him my real address, so I asked him to drop me off here. I lied. I told him I needed food to take back with me."

Darren took the gun of out Reese's back. "I don't believe your ass, but we need to talk. Let's go to the park on 51st and Racine."

"I need to find Jamal. I need to find out if he knows anything about my sister's rape."

"Yeah, that's right." Darren snapped his fingers, putting two and two together for the first time. "Tracey is your sister. I heard what happened."

"Have you heard who did it?"

"Nah, not yet, but I'll keep my ears open. So are you and Jamal close? I heard that ya used ta kick it, but you left town. He ended up fuckin' your sister."

Reese wondered where Darren was coming from.

"Ya know, Jamal coulda prevented that situation with your sister from happening."

"How?"

"Nothing happens on these streets without Jamal's knowing. He could have easily told anyone not to mess with Tracey—simple shit like that—but he treated her, his baby mother, like shit. He has no respect for her."

"Jamal has no respect for nobody except himself."

"Then why did you come back?"

"Why you being so damn nosy? That's none of your gotdamn business."

"Yeah, you right," Darren said, frustrated that he couldn't steer the conversation in the direction he wanted it to go.

"I don't give a damn. Curious, but the shit don't matter. Ya know, though, that Jamal will simply fuck you and toss y'all out like garbage."

"Not if I—"

"If you what?"

"Nothing. Where is Jamal?"

"I was going to ask you the same thing."

"I haven't talked to him. I guess I could call him."

"You got his number?"

With that, Reese began plugging numbers into her cell phone.

"Hey, Jamal," Reese said as he answered the phone, "I was wondering where you was. I came back from the hospital. Tracey is still in a coma. It's bad, Jamal. You gotta find who did this. Where are you? Why won't you tell me? When are you coming back? Oh!"

Darren was impressed. Reese had Jamal's second number. *Maybe I misjudged the depth of their relationship.* The expression on her face told him that she was disappointed with the turn the conversation had taken.

"Jamal is out of town for a couple of days," Reese said to Darren.

"Out of town? Now? Damn! That fucks up everything. He knows that we got business to take care of. Where is he?"

"He wouldn't say."

"I'm outta here."

As he watched the cars zoom by, he looked up and down the street. That's when he spotted the same black four-door Regal that brought Reese to Ashland parked halfway up the block.

Chapter Seventeen

David drove Vanessa to O'Hare Airport for her flight back to Detroit. Once he completed his mission, he vowed, he would call her.

He was sad to see her leave. She'd brought back some balance to his life. For too long he only knew anger and revenge. And the passion—that was an unexpected plus, if only for a short while. It gave him peace, knowing he was capable of something more.

He retrieved her bags from the trunk of his car, and she gave him a friendly kiss on the cheek.

"Don't be a stranger, stranger." She winked at him.

David simply smiled and watched as she disappeared through the doors of the airport.

He got back in his car and headed southbound back into the heart of downtown Chicago. He wouldn't go back to the apartment. He'd spent too much time there already, waiting for Tracey to contact him.

He considered going to John Stronger Hospital to check on Tracey's condition but quickly changed his mind. *What good would that do?* They certainly wouldn't let him in to see her, and probably would not give him any information either. It's not like he was a relative. He was out of the loop, now that Tracey was unable to give him information, and there was no one else he could turn to. He felt as though his plans were falling apart. "Shit." He pounded the steering wheel. "Man, she's got to get better."

He drove slowly through the heavy downtown traffic. His mind replayed the pieces of his plan, and how he could compensate for not having Tracey's help, but he came up empty.

David decided he needed a drink or two, maybe three, to settle his mind. He exited the expressway at 63rd Street, and thought about the local bars and lounges in the neighborhood. The only lounge that he remembered in the heart of the Englewood area was the Taste Lounge.

"Better than nothing," he said out loud as he turned onto the side street where the club was located. He noticed men and women dressed in their Sunday best walking eagerly to the front entrance of the club. Men sported suits in bright flashy colors, blood red and turquoise blue, with matching Stacy Adams'. Women wore leopard print mini skirts that looked as though they were painted on their skin, and tight-fitting halters, exposing their out-of-shape bodies.

David parked his car around the corner and walked back to the entrance of the club. The soothing sounds of steppers' music filtered in the doorway. David handed the bouncer his ten dollars cover charge.

The interior was painted a dull yellow that matched the outdated shag carpet that covered the floor.

He walked past the dance floor, where couples were engaged in the real form of *bopping* before they named it *stepping*. He found a spot at the bar, where he could watch them dance.

"May I help you?" a female bartender asked sweetly.

"Mmm," David exhaled. "Gimme *JD* on the rocks."

"Hard day, huh?"

"You don't know the half of it."

"Maybe you can tell me, sugar." She left to fill his request.

David felt several eyes looking in his direction. He graciously smiled at a few admirers—This was an older crowd—but he was not physically attracted to any one of them.

A few of the more aggressive ladies politely asked him to dance. He declined their offers, content to sit at the bar and sip on his JD and watch the crowd.

"Baby, what's your story?" the bartender asked, wiping down the counter as she spoke.

"My story?"

"All these women been asking you to dance and you've shot them down one by one."

"I don't feel like dancing."

"Can you dance? Better yet, do you know how to step?"

"No, baby, I don't step, I bop. I'm old school."

"I like that in ya, sugar. I'm taking a break in ten minutes. Do you mind if I come back and join you?"

David shrugged his shoulders. "I don't care."

"Don't sound so enthusiastic."

"I'd feel better if you buy me a drink," he said.

"That drink in your hand, sugar, is already on me."

"Really? Then I'll buy you a drink."

"I don't want to drink. Thanks anyway. I wanna dance. I want to see your fine ass move on the floor."

David blushed at her straightforwardness.

The Taste Lounge filled quickly, blocking David's view of the dance floor. The makeup of the crowd had changed from an older audience that loved to be-bop, to a younger, hip-hop crowd.

David decided to move closer to the dance floor. He found a spot in a dark corner, where he could nurse his drink, and not worry as much about women accosting him. His heart stopped when he thought he saw a familiar face on the dance floor. David squinted his eyes for clarity.

"That heifer!"

He watched Reese twist her ass on the dance floor to the lyrical rap of 50 Cent's "Candy Shop" vibrating from the speakers. His eyes held fiercely on her as she danced with an anonymous male for over ten minutes.

When the music shifted to a slower groove, she strolled off the dance floor. He traveled quickly along the wall of the lounge, keeping her in his sight.

When she found a stool at the bar, he moved in. "Whatever you order, it's on me," he said, leaning over her shoulder, looking her straight in the eye.

Reese turned to face him. "Thank you, but I ordered a glass of water." She laughed.

"Oh," was all David could say. "If you want something to drink, I'm buying." He motioned for the bartender to take their order.

"Well, since you're paying, I'll have me an Apple Martini," she informed the bartender.

"I'll have another JD."

David couldn't miss the disappointed look on the bartender's face. Reese noticed the look too.

"Old girlfriend?"

"Her?" David pointed at the bartender. "Don't know her. But may I ask your name?"

Reese studied David carefully. "Rene. My name is Rene. And yours?"

David was tempted to lie himself. "David." He extended his hand. "It's nice to meet you, Rene." He looked at her quizzically. *I wonder if I have the right woman. Is this really Rene, and not Reese?*

"Is something wrong?"

"Oh, no. It's just that you're so lovely."

"Well, thank you," she said. "And you're good-lookin' yourself."

"Do you come here often?"

"Here? Never. I was just walkin' by and heard the music. Thought I'd watch the dancing to fill some time."

"My lucky day."

David and Reese spent the next hour drinking

and talking, finally moving to the end stools at the bar for more privacy.

"So what do you do for a living?" Reese asked curiously.

"Is that the way it goes these days? The women get straight to the chase, ask the man what he does, how much money he makes, and what kind of car he drives?" There was humor in his voice, but Reese knew there was truth in his response. "Tell me, Rene, what do you do?"

"Is that how it goes? You get straight to the chase, ask me what I do, how much money I make, what kind of car I drive?"

David laughed. "I deserved that."

"I'm currently looking for a job."

"What kind of work you do?"

"I got lots of experience, mostly customer service, some office work, filing, answering phone, stuff like that."

"Mmm, that's interesting. I have my own business, a printing company," David lied, "and I'm looking for a receptionist. Let me hear your telephone voice."

"Are you serious?"

"Are you serious about a job?"

"Hello, this is Rene Adams. May I help you?" She looked directly at David.

He bit his lips. *I'm not letting this bitch leave my eyesight.* "That's good, damn good. The job is yours, if you want it."

Reese looked at him doubtfully. "That was my interview? Just like that? That shit is too good to be true. How much you gon' pay me?"

"Wooooooo, slow down, sweetheart. First, you

doubt me, and now you want to know how much you're getting paid. First things first. I'm going to give you my info." David searched his wallet for his business card. "Must be out. Gotta get new cards printed. Here"—He slid a napkin across the table—"put your name and contact number on this." He wrote down his name and number on another napkin. "Maybe we can get together tomorrow and take care of the details, but tonight I want to chill. Want to dance?"

Reese nodded her head. "Yes."

As David led Reese by the arm towards the dance floor, he looked up to see the bartender frowning at him. *If you only knew, if you only knew.*

They danced, drank, and talked until the club announced they were closing.

"Hungry?" he asked. "I'm not ready for the evening to end."

"Uh-huh," she said, "but I don't know about going with you."

"I'm taking my chances too, you know. Women are as fuckin' crazy as men."

Reese laughed.

"Look, my car is parked around the corner. We can go somewhere close by, order breakfast or whatever you like, and I can take you home."

"You not taking me home. That's not going down."

"Fine, it's your call. You said you're hungry, so let's get something to eat and call it a night."

"I don't know," she said reluctantly. "There's a restaurant down the street. We can go there."

"Can we sit down?"

"Yeah, of course."

Reese shared with David that she lived in Detroit and Chicago, but said nothing about her sister.

Something about David seemed familiar. His eyes? Voice? His general demeanor? Reese couldn't pinpoint whatever it was. Anyway, she enjoyed his company, but not enough to disclose her true name.

"So you lived in Detroit? Where?"

"Not *in* Detroit, but *near* Detroit," she said.

"Okay. Where?"

His probing made her nervous. "Look, I just met you. I don't usually tell my life story on the first night. Besides, you haven't told me nothin' about you."

"Okay, okay. Fair. I really don't have family. My mother and brother died in the same year, and my father died when I was a child. So it's basically me. I mean, I have cousins and stuff, but it's nothing like your immediate family. You know that connection— mother, father, brother or sister. I wish I had a sister. Do you have any siblings?" he asked, happy to get these questions out so easily.

"Rene?" David could see Reese mentally draw away from the conversation.

Reese jumped. "Huh?"

"Nothing. I see that your mind is somewhere else. Can I take you somewhere after you finish eating, drop you off somewhere?"

"How about your crib?" Reese stroked David intimately betweens the thighs.

"My crib? Cool."

He wasn't sure he meant it when he pulled out of the parking spot. His plans did not include a sexual relationship with his prey. He remembered the condoms in his glove compartment.

Reese continued to caress David, her hands smoothly moving up and down his thigh area, reaching his groin. *Maybe I can knock this fool up for some money, and have a quick place to stay until I take care of Jamal. This fool don't know what's hit him.* She reached for David's penis, feeling it harden under her hand massage.

Chapter Eighteen

Jamal entered downtown Detroit minutes before midnight. His fuel light was on, so he pulled into the first station he saw, a Mobil, before meeting Charlene at her motel. As he pulled up to an available pump, another SUV, the same color as his, pulled up behind him, its music blaring from the speakers. Jamal looked up to see a male driver with a bunch of young females barely over the age of 16 in the front and back seats. When one of the young girls winked at him, he blushed and licked his lips in a flirtatious gesture.

Seeing this, another girl winked too. The girls giggled and laughed with abandon. The driver seemed irritated. He asked one of the girls in the front a question, but she was too preoccupied with Jamal. He punched her arm, causing her to look away from Jamal to him.

"Ouch!"

"Bitch, your attention should be on me, not that muthafucka out there."

Jamal, hearing the exchange of words, continued to pump his gas.

The driver jumped out of his SUV, his motor still running. He gave Jamal a hateful look, and then narrowed his eyes in recognition. He walked up on Jamal. "Dude, I know you."

Jamal stood back, his hand tucked under his shirt. "Yeah, you do look familiar."

"You from these parts?"

"Nah." Jamal returned his attention to the pump, hoping the dude would go back to his car.

"Cat, what's your name?"

"Man, you don't need to know my muthafuckin' name. I don't live here."

"Your nigga ass from Chi-town." The driver spotted Jamal's license plate. "Jun-Jun! That's it, you Jun-Jun's muthafuckin' brother, Jamal, right?"

"Yeah." Jamal still didn't place the young man's name or face.

"Rico, dawg. I was your brother's hook-up man."

"Damn, that's right." Jamal snapped his fingers. "Man, we need to talk."

"Yeah, I haven't heard from my dawg, Jun-Jun. Wha' gives?"

"J-J-Jun-Jun," Jamal stuttered, his voice filling with emotion, "Jun-Jun been popped."

"Straight up?" Rico cupped his mouth, surprised he didn't hear about it. "Man, that's foul. I'm sorry to hear that, dawg. That was my muthafuckin' nigga. Damn!"

"When and where can we talk?" Jamal asked seriously.

"We can go back to my crib," Rico told him, still wrestling with the news about Jun-Jun, a bro he really liked. "I live about five minutes from here."

"And the bitches . . . ?"

"They're going too, but they won't be in the way."

"Man, what type of business are you in? Big car, dime pieces . . ."

"The oldest business on this muthafuckin' planet." Rico jumped back in his SUV.

Jamal followed Rico through the streets of Detroit to Rico's apartment complex. He watched the five females bounce from the SUV and follow Rico in lock step to his apartment. Jamal walked behind, surveying the parking lot and building entrance. He walked into Rico's small but neatly furnished two-bedroom apartment.

Rico motioned for Jamal to wait for him in the living room. Rico escorted the girls into the second bedroom, closed the door, and locked it with a chain fastener.

Jamal laughed. "Dawg, is it that serious?"

"Man, that's my bread and butter. Hell yeah, it's that serious. Gotta keep 'em in line."

"A'ight, you're a muthafuckin' 2005 pimp. How you keep the bitches in their place?"

"Rules," Rico said. "My first rule of the game is that I get them young and dumb. Not one of them is over sixteen years old. Runaways, state wards, and shit, they stay here." He pointed to his apartment. "It's better than the shit where they came from. I feed their asses, clothe them, shit, ya know. The younger, the better. Easier to handle. They not fucked up on that shit. And the muthafuckin' johns love the young pussy. You know what I mean?"

"Yeah, yeah. Your game tight, dawg, but I need to get some weight, and quick."

"How quick we talkin' 'bout? I'm trying to get out of that line of work. The heat is too muthafuckin' hot these days."

"And your shit?"

"These bitches are fucked up in the head. When they start to give me trouble, I let their asses go, kick their asses out. They usually beg to come back, but by that time they is yesterday's news—garbage. I find me some new pussy to play with."

Jamal was growing impatient. "Mmmmm . . . can you hook me up or what?"

"Give me a couple of hours. I have to make a few calls. Some weight, huh? What we talkin' 'bout? You need a few kilos, or do you need a brick, what?"

"As much as you can get as quick as possible." Jamal stood to leave. "Got a number to be reached at?"

"Bet, dawg." Rico wrote down his number. "Hit me up on my cellie. I'll have some news for you about twelve noon tomorrow. That's cool?"

"Cool." Jamal shut the door.

Jamal called Charlene on the phone to get the directions to her motel. She informed him that she was at Carmichael's apartment, not at the motel.

"Jamal," Charlene said, "he ain't here, you know that. So, baby, come on over."

Jamal, feeling the drain from his long drive, didn't want to argue. Reluctantly, he drove to Carmichael's apartment. He parked his SUV near the front entrance of the building. He looked around the area and activated his alarm. *My shit better not get stolen.*

He looked up and smiled to see Charlene standing at the window. She buzzed him in and ran into the hallway, her arms open wide.

Crazy ol' shit.

"Baby, you made it safe. Thank you, Jesus."

As much as he loved Charlene, she could embarrass him with all her hugging and cheek-pinching. "I'm fine, and tired."

"Come on in. I'll fix the couch up for you, open a can of soup. I have to admit, your fa—I mean, Carmichael is a filthy slob. He has stuff everywhere."

"I'm not surprised," Jamal said. "The muthafucka never took care of anything but himself."

"Jamal!"

"It's true, and you know it."

He dropped his bag on the floor near the couch and flopped down on the sofa, but not before shoveling dirty socks, old newspapers, dried bread crusts, along with a pile of unwashed clothes to the floor.

He grabbed the remote control. "I hope this cheap-ass muthafucka have cable," he said quietly.

"Jamal, I know you got a lot of hatred for Carmichael, and I understand where you comin' from, but, baby, your—Carmichael is gravely ill. They don't think he's going to make it."

"What happened, anyway? Not that I care." He flipped through the channels, only half-listening to Charlene.

"I told you they said he was drinking and driving. Carmichael loves that bottle. I wanted to come over here to see if he had any papers, or something, insurance papers, a bank account, or something."

"Yeah, do this muthafucka have insurance? And if he dies, who will inherit his shit? Like he got some shit to get. Maybe I can get that stale hot dog bun . . . ya think?"

"Jamal, here are some boxes. I got 'em from his closet. Here, help me carry them."

"Charlene, I'm tired. I don't feel like looking through his shit." Jamal tossed the box on the floor, spilling the contents onto the carpet.

Old bills, pictures, newspaper clippings scattered across the room. Jamal looked down at a photo of men and women in sexually compromising positions. He laughed out loud when he spotted a snapshot of a naked Carmichael and a naked woman.

He stooped to pick it up. That's when he saw a photo of Carmichael in a sexual position with another man. "This was a dirty, freaky muthafucka."

Jamal lifted the batch of pictures and sifted through them, disgusted that this man's blood ran through his. He stopped abruptly when he recognized a woman in one of the shots—Reese, naked and spread-eagled on a bed.

Chapter Nineteen

"Paula, have you heard from Joe?" the sergeant asked as he strolled past her desk.

"Nope, not a word." She continued typing.

"That's not good. What about the girl?"

Paula shrugged. "Hey, Operation Substitute is scratched."

"Joe didn't agree to it though. He could still be out there trying to keep it alive."

"Well, he was told. I can't help it if he can't follow orders. We're moving to the next plan."

"Get me a list of the gang members, and anything you have on them. We'll conduct a sweep, hell, bring their asses in on spitting violations if we have to. We got to do something. City Hall is riding my ass."

"I'm all on it. Joe is gonna be pissed, but he had his chance. That fuckin' addict blew it."

"Call him then. Tell him to get his ass in here."

"Will do."

Paula watched the sergeant leave the office, his head down, burdened by the pressure to act, do anything, to tell the powers-that-be that he was making progress.

She dialed Joe's cell phone, fully expecting him to ignore the call.

Joe saw Paula's number on his caller ID. "Yeah, whatcha want?"

"Joe, it's Paula. You comin' in the office? We have to talk about the new operation."

"No, not until tomorrow. I'm trying to move ahead on this. I know Sarge is ready to pull the plug—"

"No, not *ready*. The plug has been pulled, and you know that."

"Listen, I got a good lead, a damn good lead, and possibly some heavy shit that will put the top layer of the Hustlers in jail. I'm seriously thinking about putting a wire on Reese, and—"

The phone conversation was prematurely disconnected.

"Joe? Joe?" *Let him go through with the plan, the dumb committed muthafucka. It's his damn job on the line.*

She shuffled through her paperwork collected on the Cobras and Hustlers. She knew the officers that would be assigned to conduct the sweep. In fact, she had an intimate relationship with the leading investigator.

"Angelo," Paula said.

"Princess, how are you?"

"Shit's burning. The heat's going down in the street."

"I heard, I heard," he said. "I tried to put the word out for everyone to be cool."

"Good," Paula said. "Look, your unit will probably be assigned to conduct the sweep on the Hustlers. Their asses haven't paid up, so we need a damn good sweep, understand?"

"Yeah, I read you. We want sticky shit."

"You got it." She laughed. "But by the book, baby."

"Nothing but."

Chapter Twenty

Darren saw a line of police cars driving westbound on 63rd Street and ran into the West Englewood Library. Until he knew what was going down, the library was a quiet and inconspicuous spot to chill. He walked to the back, where the magazines were located, and sat in a seat in the corner. He browsed through several African American publications, including *Honey*, *Upscale*, *Ebony*, and *Black Enterprise*, scattered on a table.

He looked around the nearly empty library. He thumped his fingers on the table, trying to decide his next step. He knew he was a dead man. News that he'd turned on his main man would be on the streets in no time, but not, he hoped, before Jamal got what he deserved for killing his nephew.

Darren flipped through the latest *Chicago Tribune* and came across a commentary regarding his nephew, Anthony Paxton, written by Lisa Stillman:

VICTIMS OF A VIOLENT SOCIETY, OUR CHILDREN NO
LONGER HAVE A CHILDHOOD.

Darren ripped the commentary out of the newspaper and stuffed it in his pocket. He exited the library in a rush, with a new determination.

He flagged a cab, tossing the driver a fifty-dollar
bill through the glass plate window, and instructed
him to go to Alsip, Illinois, where his sister stayed
with her boyfriend.

The cabdriver tried to make small talk as they
rode to the far south suburb of Chicago.

"Man, don't say shit to me, a'ight? Just get me to
my destination."

"Yes, sir," the man answered with a strong foreign
accent. "I meant no harm."

Darren looked out the window, refusing to comment.

The cabdriver weaved in and out of Chicago's
traffic, accelerating his speed to get Darren to his
destination as soon as possible.

They arrived in Alsip with change to spare. Darren hopped out of the cab and waved the driver on.
The cabbie drove off with a twenty-dollar tip, relieved that the angry black male was out of his vehicle.

Darren walked up to apartment complex 2104
and rang the doorbell.

"Who is it?" asked a husky male voice.

"Kevin, is Angela there?"

"She doesn't want to talk to you," he replied
through the intercom.

"Man, don't fuckin' play with me. Let me talk to
my sister," Darren demanded.

When the buzzer sounded, Darren opened the door and walked to the third floor of the apartment complex.

"You got a lot of nerve coming here," Kevin said. "I told you your sister don't want to speak to you. I'm gonna let you in, but be cool. We got company." He instructed Darren to follow him to a bedroom.

As he passed the entry to the living room, Darren spotted his sister on the couch, her face stained with tears, talking to a young lady dressed in a navy blue suit. He could only see her profile, but he didn't think he recognized her.

When Angela looked up to see him standing there, he froze. Her angry eyes held him rooted to the floor.

"I truly appreciate you granting me this interview, Ms. Paxton. The public needs to know what our young children have to face on a daily basis. My columns about children being victims of violent crimes have tried to personalize this problem. Thank you for your help. Anthony's story touched so many hearts. That's why I'm here. I guess I just want you to know how many people have identified with you. But I won't stop writing about the plight of Englewood. I still live there, and the gang violence is out of control."

"What more can you do?" Angela asked.

"Well, I plan to do extensive research about gangs, even get inside, see how they work."

"Well, when you start to write about gangs, that's the person you need to talk to." She pointed at Darren. "He's a gang banger for the Hustlers, a killer. The same damn gang that killed my son." Her voice was uncharacteristically calm, the finger pointing at him steady.

Lisa stood to look at Darren.

"Hello, my name is Lisa Stillman. I write for the *Chicago Tribune*. Here is my card. I would love to talk to you in depth."

Darren tossed the card on the floor.

Lisa picked it back up and handed it back to him. "Think about it, please. I'll keep your identity concealed. I simply want information."

"What kind of information?"

"Whatever you want to provide," she said.

"Mmmm . . . when are you available?"

"We can set up an appointment."

"Nah, I don't have time for that. If you want information, I can talk to you now. But if—"

"Now is cool," Lisa said eagerly. "Let me finish with your sister, and we can talk. I got all the time you need."

"Now if I give you this information, what exactly are you going to do for me?"

"I don't know. What do you want?"

"A deal."

Darren stepped into the living room, taking small, tentative steps towards his sister. He slowly eased his body down next to her, fully expecting her to block him. When she didn't, he sighed. "I don't trust the police, and I don't trust you."

"What kind of mess was Carmichael involved in, taking these naked pictures of men and women?" Charlene looked over Jamal's shoulders at the pile of pictures.

"He's a muthafuckin' faggot."

"Jamal! Please have a little respect for me, okay. Your language is hard on my ears." Charlene covered her ears with her hands.

Jamal picked up the naked picture of Reese.

"Oh my, isn't that the young lady you brought to the restaurant?" she asked.

"Yeah, that's the nasty b—ho. I can't believe this ho slept with Carmichael. Ain't that a bitch!"

"Jamal!" Charlene said.

"Oops, sorry," he said, trying to keep the annoyance out of his voice.

"You know, I forgot to tell you," Charlene said, "but when y'all was at the restaurant, that girl was in the bathroom talking on her phone to someone, saying that she was with you. And I heard her say your name, and she used that word, you know, she said you were a . . ."

"A what, Charlene? Just spit it out."

"Right. She said—mind you, I'm only repeating what she said—she said, 'that muthafucka Jamal.' "

"Really? You heard that, huh?"

"Mmmm-hmm." Charlene took a second look at Reese in the photo. "She's nasty."

Chapter Twenty-one

Reese woke the next morning on David's couch, wearing his T-shirt. She glanced at the time on the DVD player and noticed that it was close to noon. She sat up on the couch and looked around the room.

The living room in the one-bedroom apartment looked tired, certainly not prosperous. It contained a sofa, a small entertainment center that held a 27-inch color television, and a coffee table. The white walls were bare, no personal mementos or artifacts anywhere.

Reese could see the kitchen area from where she sat, and she noted that the countertops were bare. Thirsty, she got up from the couch and walked to the refrigerator to get something to drink, but, except for a pitcher of water, it was completely empty. Curiously, she opened the cabinets and counted on one hand the numbers of plates, glasses, and bowls. No soup cans, snacks, nothing.

She grabbed a clean plastic cup and poured herself a glass of water.

David, fully dressed, walked into the kitchen with Reese. "Good afternoon."

"Yeah, good afternoon. Do you really live here?"

"Why would you ask me something like that?"

"Because it's bare—no food, no photos, nothing that would tell me who you are. I couldn't even tell you what cereal you eat. You have three plates, one glass, two plastic cups, and two bowls."

"Why are you taking inventory of my stuff? I extended my sofa to you, and you're rumbling through my kitchen cabinets?"

"I'm sorry. Thank you for your couch, but I would have rather slept in your bed." She moved in closer to him.

"My bed, huh?" He pushed her away.

"What's wrong with you? Your dick got hard—I noticed that in the car—but you rejected me last night, and you're dissin' me today. What gives? You do like women, don't you?"

David laughed. "Just because I don't want to freak you, I must be gay, is that it?"

"You brought me back to your apartment."

"And you came with me."

"I thought that—"

"Don't think, okay, because you will never guess the right answer." He walked to his stove to put on a pot of water. "Coffee?"

"So you don't have no family?" She leaned against the wall and watched David make himself a cup of coffee. Everything about him appeared mysterious to her now.

"I thought I told you that. My brother and

mother died the same year. And you, Rene, what about your family?"

"What happened to your brother and mother?" Reese asked.

"My mother died of a heart attack" And then, in an almost off-handed voice, he added, "And my brother, he was murdered." He watched Reese for her reaction and was surprised when her eyes misted from his confession.

"I know how it feels to lose someone," she said finally. "My sister is in the hospital now, fighting for her life. Maybe you saw it on TV. She was the latest victim of that rapist." She walked to the living area and plopped on the sofa. "She's gotta make it. I deserted her, and I owe her so much, so much. I have so much to prove to her."

David took a deep breath. He had finally brought the conversation around to where he needed it to go, but he had to be slow. He needed to show patience and concern. Anything less could push her away. "Oh, Rene, how terrible for you. I know how it is to face this kind of thing alone. I've been there, and it's hell. Do they have him yet, the rapist?"

"They think it's a serial rapist. If I catch the muthafucka, I'm gonna kill him for doing that to her." She took a deep breath.

"That's the way I feel about my brother's killers. I could just kill those muthafuckas." He stared bitterly at Reese.

She heard the pain dripping from his voice, but she couldn't see him through the tears blurring her vision. She couldn't see the hatred in his eyes.

Chapter Twenty-two

Lisa pulled a tape recorder from her bag, and grabbed a pen and pad. They had moved from the living room to the kitchen table, where Kevin and Angela promised them privacy.

Darren feared that his sister could overhear the interview and hate him even more, if that was possible, but she reassured him that neither she nor Kevin had any interest in bringing further anger or pain on themselves.

"Hey! I ain't talkin' in no tape recorder," Darren said. "You can take as many notes as you need, but—"

"No problem." Lisa quickly deposited her recorder back into her briefcase. "I want you to be comfortable. Whatever works. I'm flexible." She paused. "So how long have you been in a gang?"

"For over ten years."

"And what made you join a gang?"

"I didn't look at it as *joining*. I mean, I grew with

my boys, we hung out together, fought together, got drunk together. We had each other's back. We's family."

"Yeah, I heard that theory before. We're family, looking out for one another. Family don't kill one another."

"Are you going to listen or pass judgment? I don't need this bullshit."

"I'm sorry." *What am I thinking?* Lisa knew better. After all, it was her responsibility to be objective, not throw in critical comments that didn't serve the interview. "This gang issue, the killing, is a sore spot with me. I'm sorry. I truly appreciate that you're sharing your story with me. I don't mean to be judgmental."

"The gang is a family. They're there when your damn family is not."

"Mmmm . . . I can understand that, but how do you justify the killings?"

"Again, if someone messes with your family member, you hurt them back—an eye for an eye—shit, it's the law of the streets. It's written in the Bible."

"But innocent victims are being killed. How do you rationalize that?"

"I don't," he said softly. "It's a part of the territory. I don't like it, but . . ."

"Your sister said that your gang killed your nephew."

Darren looked down at his hands. "Look, if I share this information with you, I'm putting myself in danger. Most times, I don't give a damn. I know that I'm a dead man. But by sharing this with you, you will be putting yourself out there too." He watched Lisa weigh her options. "I have also shared this information with others that maybe I shouldn't have."

"Like?"

"A rival gang."

"Why?"

"Revenge."

"Hey, let me call a friend on the police force. Maybe he could give me some info on how best to help you."

"No, no," Darren told her. "No cops."

"But you want a deal. That's what you said in your sister's living room."

"I don't know what I want." He slumped down in the chair, his mind and body exhausted. "I should kill Jamal and get this shit over with."

"Why do you want to kill Jamal?" She wrote the name down in her notebook.

"Because he ordered my nephew killed," Darren told her.

"Have you ever killed anyone?"

"I'm not answering that question. Next!"

Chapter Twenty-three

Reese's hands trembled when she saw the incoming call from Joe. She knew she could only avoid his phone calls for a period of time before he started to look for her again. She needed to get to Jamal somehow and hand him over to Joe, to finally finish the job and get him off her back. She surprised herself that she'd been able to get through the last day without scrambling for crack, but she was still exhausted. If she could only sit with her sister and nurse her back to health, make up for her neglect.

Another call came in on her cell phone. It was from Jamal.

"Hey," she said, feigning excitement.

"I need to see you," Jamal said. "I'm coming back to the city tonight, and we need to get together. Where are you?"

"On my way to the hospital," she lied.

"I'll be back 'round eight this evening. Meet me at Sam's Spot on 62nd and Aberdeen."

"Cool. No problem. Where you comin' back from?"

"None of your gotdamn business! Just be there at eight or else . . ."

The "or else" frightened Reese, tempting her to skip the date, but then she remembered Joe. She knew she had no choice. When would it end?

Jamal called Rico to check on his order, but got his voicemail instead. "Damn," he said out loud. *That muthafucka better come through.* He got up from the couch and walked towards the kitchen, where Charlene was frying bacon and eggs.

"That smells good." He rubbed his stomach.

"It's almost ready. After I'm finished, I'm going up to the hospital to check on Carmichael. Why don't—"

"I'm not going to see that fool, Charlene. He can die, for all I care. I need to get back to Chicago to take care of some unfinished business."

"Oh, Jamal, you shouldn't talk like that. I know that he wasn't the best, but I don't want him to die."

The sadness in her voice made Jamal regret his words.

"I wish you would stay and go see him."

"Nah, Charlene, I have to get back, seriously. But I ain't going to leave until I eat your good cookin'."

Happy to have someone to cook for, Charlene smiled. She wiped her hands on her apron. "Sit down, boy, and get some of this breakfast in your belly." She placed the plate of bacon and eggs on the table.

"I need to call the hospital. Yes, mmmm-hmm." Charlene mumbled as she walked about the kitchen, cleaning and putting items back into the cupboard.

"I need to be transferred to the nurse's station," she said. "Yes, this is she. Oh no, my God." When she dropped the phone to the floor, Jamal turned to look at her.

"Carmichael just died, sugar, an hour ago," she said, crying.

Jamal sucked on his teeth to remove a piece of bacon. "I gotta go, Charlene," he said, ignoring Charlene's news and her obvious pain. "Call me if you need more money." He dropped five hundred dollars on the kitchen counter. *That fool deserved to die.*

Reese convinced David to take her to Evergreen Plaza, hoping she could suck him out of some money, and David went along with the game, wanting to keep her near until he could figure out his next move.

He knew Reese saw him as gullible, and perhaps under other conditions, he could have been. Reese, he admitted to himself, was attractive, perhaps too aggressive, but nevertheless, he liked looking at her. He laughed that they were both playing each other, but only he knew that, and that gave him all the cards. Her moves were so transparent that, at times, he found it hard to maintain the look of sympathy that she seemed to appreciate on his face.

When she asked him to help her buy an outfit, he agreed, but only if she agreed to buy something sexy and model it—among other things. He liked that she thought of him as a susceptible male, one she could manipulate and fleece out of his money. That only worked in his favor. And when she asked if she could crash at his spot for a couple more days, stating that she'd been temporarily staying at her sister's place—a real hellhole—until she found a better one for herself, he jumped at the idea. Keeping her close to him reinvigorated his plans.

But Reese continued to be bothered. There was something about David that she couldn't put her hands on. He was too easy-going, too convincing, and too damn nice. *Too damn bad.* She laughed.

Reese and David walked across Evergreen Plaza parking lot, lost in their own thoughts. She decided not to get anything too extravagant, not this first time out.

David thought about her phone call. He wanted to know who she called. He overheard her say, "Eight." *Is she meeting someone then?* If so, he prayed it was Jamal.

Reese and David walked through the mall, gazing in the store windows.

Reese admired a pair of white Jordan's. "They're nice."

"Yeah, but I don't want you to model no damn Jordan's. How about that over there?" He pointed in the direction of a lingerie store, where a mannequin in the window sported a red thong with a matching red see-thru bikini top.

"Mmmm, that will look nice with the white Jordan's, or even better with high-heel sneakers."

David looked at the new high-heeled gym shoes and shook his head. "I don't think so."

David and Reese walked in the direction of the lingerie shop. Reese playfully bumped into him, knocking him off his balance. He responded in kind.

Reese liked that he had a playful way, an easy demeanor that she enjoyed being around. This was new for her. She tried to think of another man that she'd had in her life who'd allowed her the freedom to be herself, no abuse, no anger, no controlling attitude.

It felt good, but more than that, it felt normal.

David took her hand as they walked. He felt his stomach rumble. "Wanna get a bite to eat at Applebee's when we finish? I'm starved."

Reese squeezed his hand. "Sure." She smiled to herself. *So normal.* She looked across the mall and saw other couples walking together, talking, holding hands.

Reese purchased the red lingerie outfit, a jogging suit, and two pair of shoes, including her high-heeled sneakers.

They walked hand in hand out of Evergreen Plaza shopping mall, David carrying her packages for her. The two were talking, making plans. First, they would eat then go back to the apartment for Reese to change clothes. She told him she wanted to go to the hospital, and he offered to drive her.

Lost in conversation, they didn't see Joe until they literally bumped into him as he opened his car door.

"Joe?" David said. "Man, how are you?"

Joe looked surprised at the sight of Reese and

David together, holding hands. "David, it's been a while. How's Detroit treating you?"

Reese looked suspiciously at David and then back at Joe, signaling him not to recognize her.

"Man, I'm back in Chicago. Have been for a quite some time," he said, avoiding the question. David watched Reese from the corner of his eye. He didn't want Joe to disclose that he was a cop. "I've got a printing business going and—"

Joe looked at Reese. "So you're no longer on the police force?"

"Man, I'm sorry for being rude. This here is Rene. Rene, this is a friend from way back—Joe."

Joe and Reese shook hands, neither giving a clue that they knew each other.

"Nice to meet you, Rene." Joe smiled. "Pretty girl, David."

Reese blushed.

"So, man, how's the force?"

"Man, I'm not doing that no more. Got my own business, doing my own thang."

"Great. It's always good to be the *HNIC* (Head Nigga In Charge). Hey, did you ever get any resolution on your brother's death?" Joe asked innocently.

When Joe saw David's nervousness, he quickly understood that something was going down. He needed time to piece it together, but he was certain it involved Reese. He didn't like it.

"Nah, man. Look, we gotta go," David said. "We're going over to Applebee's to grab something to eat. It was good seeing you, man."

"Call me, dawg." Joe handed David his business card. "Since you're back in the city, maybe we can get together."

David took the card and put it in his wallet.

Reese continued to look at the ground as she listened uneasily to the exchange between the two men, avoiding Joe's eyes.

As they walked away, Reese looked back to see Joe rooted to the same spot, watching them, a look of revulsion written on his face.

David and Reese walked into Applebee's, the earlier happy-go-lucky mood replaced by an unspoken tension. Neither of them said a word since leaving Joe standing in the parking lot.

Reese felt her cell phone vibrate through her purse. *It's got to be Joe.* She decided to contact him later, tell him about her planned meeting with Jamal. She didn't want to explain why she was with David. That was her business, after all, none of his. Wasn't she entitled to privacy?

Once the waitress seated David and Reese in a booth off in a corner and handed them both menus, Reese said, "You didn't tell me that you was a cop." She tried to sound lighthearted.

"Because I'm not."

"And you didn't tell me that you was from Detroit."

"Because I'm not." David pretended to check out the selection on the menus. "Mmm, the T-bone steak sounds good with a house salad. How 'bout you?"

"I don't know," Reese said cheerfully. "I could eat everything on this menu."

"Since you're asking me all of these questions,"— David placed his menu down—"Where do you know Joe from?"

"I don't know Joe," she replied too quickly.

"You sure? I mean, you tried really hard to avoid eye contact with him. And your body language—"

"I-I-I didn't want to interrupt the conversation."

"Mmmm . . . anyway, what ya ordering?"

Reese pretended to study the menu, wondering what gave her away. Did she convince him that she didn't know Joe? When she looked up, she had her answer. His eyes burned with unanswered questions.

But she had questions too. The Joe-David connection disturbed her.

"I'll take a chicken sandwich with fries." She tossed the menu down on the table and folded her arms across her chest.

"Where's the damn waitress?" David said, not trying to hide his impatience.

Reese knew that it wasn't only the waitress that brought on his irritation.

"She's already starting off by not getting a damn tip. Shit, a man's hungry."

"What was your brother's name?" Reese asked.

David pounded his fist on the table. "Look, you're asking too many damn questions that're none of your gotdamn business. My brother is dead, okay. Am I asking you a hundred and one questions about your sister being raped? Did I ask if she was a prostitute or strung out on drugs, huh? Or why you were so willing to go with me after the Taste. Is that your M.O.? Let's just fuckin' eat our meal, okay."

David looked up to see Reese's face about to collapse into tears. This angered him even more, because he saw that he cared.

"I'm sorry," Reese replied above a whisper. "I

never meant . . ." She allowed the words to dissolve in the air. She hit a sore spot with him, and he retaliated by puncturing a painful spot in her heart, mentioning her sister.

I wonder how she's doing? she asked herself.

Chapter Twenty-four

Lisa drove home excited about the story suddenly dropped in her lap, but she also was beginning to realize the potential danger ahead—one that would threaten her safety. Her information was hot. She was not just interviewing a prominent gang member, but his testimony, his story, could solve a heated murder case, and not just one. Darren accused Jamal, one of the most feared individuals on the streets of Chicago. The dynamics of this story was a journalist's dream. The rewards could elevate her career to new heights, and possible nomination for the exclusive Apple Award, a highly regarded award in journalism. Or the consequences could be catastrophic. Lisa had a lot to think about.

Darren understood that, by talking to her, he was putting a target on his back, but she would do everything possible not to contribute to his danger. That she would aid in bringing a murderer to justice gave her a high, but believing that she could bring about change in her community was the biggest bonus for her. Adrenaline pulsed through her veins, making it difficult to think rationally about her next step. Placing a call to her friend would help ground her and also give her the information she felt she lacked.

"Hello, Joe," Lisa said.

"Hey," he answered.

"This is Lisa. How are you?"

"Hey, baby, I'm fine, and you?"

"Joe, I need some serious info from you. I have this potential lead for a ground-breaking story, and I need some preliminary advice ASAP."

"Chasin' another story, huh?"

"No, seriously," she replied. "This is the one, with a capital O."

"What ya want to know, Ms. Lisa?"

"If someone has information on a murder, could they plea-bargain or get a lesser charge, if they're willing to talk? What are the steps?"

"Someone has information about a murder? Are they involved? Are they trying to save their own ass? They might not have a foot to stand on."

"If they're not involved in this murder, but not clean in other areas, could they strike a deal?"

"Anything is possible. What you got?"

"A member of the Hustlers is willing to share information about who is responsible for Anthony Paxton's death."

"Wow! Be careful, Lisa. He might be using you for his own gain. I don't know about this one. What's in it for him?"

"Nothing, really. He wants to clear his conscience, I guess. He already knows that his days are numbered."

"Yeah, just make sure that *your* days are not numbered with his. You know that if you want more specific information, I'll need more details . . . like, who is your confidant, and who he wants to nail."

"I know, but I'm not ready to disclose his identity. He's just starting to trust me, and my window of time to help him is small."

"Be careful, Lisa. You might be out of your league on this one."

"Maybe, maybe not, but it's a story of a lifetime."

"Yeah, but your life is not worth a byline in the news."

"Joe, I hear you, really, and I will be careful, I promise." She wished she had the assurance behind her words.

"Okay, kiddo, just keep me informed."

Jamal met Rico at a run-down duplex two blocks away from the Mobil gas station. He usually delegated the task of picking up such large quantities of cocaine to his workers. So much was going down in his life, turning to shit, he only hoped this wouldn't be another thing. He didn't like to admit he was nervous about anything, but he was.

He knocked on the door. The blinds on the door were partially open, so he tried to peep through them. Jamal saw an older lady walking around in the house, ignoring his knock. He pressed his head closer to the window and noticed that she wore a jumper/short outfit that was unbuttoned, exposing her sagging breasts.

He knocked on the door again.

"Comin', dammit," the female voice shouted. "Hold on to your shit."

Jamal folded his arms and rocked from side to side. He was about to knock a third time when he heard a car pull up in front of the house.

Rico jumped out of the driver's seat.

"What's up, dawg?" Jamal threw up his hands. "You got the shit?"

Rico ignored Jamal and ran up the steps of the porch empty-handed.

"Let's take this conversation inside." Rico bent down to insert the key into the lock. He opened the door and walked into the cluttered house. Jamal followed.

"Sit down." Rico disappeared into another room.

"I'd rather stand. I don't have much time," Jamal said to Rico's back, clearly irritated that this wasn't going as smoothly as it should.

"Hey, baby," the older lady said as she entered the room. Her jumper, still unbuttoned, gapped in front, exposing her loose breasts, causing Jamal to pull back, disgusted.

Is she actually flirting with me?

"Sit down, honey." When she smiled at him, he saw her teeth, or the few that were left, and they were rotting on the stem.

"Rico," Jamal called out, "what the hell is going on? I have to get back to Chicago!"

Rico reappeared in the living room.

Jamal, still standing, noticed that the older lady had lit a cigarette and made herself comfortable on the couch.

"You got the money?" Rico asked.

Jamal removed his backpack and dropped it on the floor. "You got my shit? And who in the hell is this bitch?" Jamal pointed at the older lady. "I—"

His statement was interrupted by a knocking at the back door.

"Hold up." Rico backed away to answer it.

Jamal thought Rico seemed edgy, too jumpy for what should be an easy transaction. He leaned over to watch Rico open the back door and invite several males into the house. He became alarmed and made a quick dial on his cell phone, wondering if he should just hightail it out of there while he still could. He heard the exchange of voices, but they were purposely kept low.

After several minutes, when no one had appeared, Jamal called out, "Man, I'm outta here. You got som'n' goin' down." He walked to the window and spotted two black sedans pulling up in front of the house. He smiled.

Rico came back into the living room with the three males. "These here are my boys," Rico explained to Jamal.

"I don't give a fuck who they are. Do you have my shit?"

"I have to count the money before we make the exchange." Rico motioned for one of his boys to retrieve the backpack.

Jamal put his foot on the bag, stopping him from picking it up. "Hell nah. Your ass trippin'."

Rico pulled out a pistol and stuck it to Jamal's head. "What if I just take your damn money? What your punk ass goin' to do about it?"

Jamal didn't flinch at the sight of the gun. He

looked Rico square in the eyes. "You sure you want to play like this?" Jamal asked, his voice in full control. "I'm not no nickel-and-dime dealer you're fuckin' with."

"I don't care who the fuck you are." Rico slammed the butt of the gun against Jamal's head. "I can kill your ass right here. You ain't in Chicago—"

Before Rico could finish his statement, he heard loud banging on the front door. "Who the fuck is that?" He looked at Jamal and then at his boys.

"Look out the window," Jamal told him.

Before Rico could make a move, the front door was kicked in.

"Detroit Police! Drop your weapons and freeze!"

Rico dropped his gun on the floor and attempted to kick it under the couch. His boys lifted their hands in the air.

Jamal walked behind the officers and smiled. He picked the pistol up off the floor. "Officers, I think you'll need this as evidence." He took the gun and stuck it in Rico's mouth. "Now, who's the punk ass?"

Rico's eyes darted back and forth from Jamal to the police officers.

"What do you want us to do with them?" one officer asked.

Jamal looked at the four frightened men and chuckled. "This muthafucka here was going to try and rob me. And you said that you was Jun-Jun's boy. Fuck these muthafuckas up, and then let them go. But him . . . kill him."

"No, Jamal, man," Rico pleaded, tears gushing down his face. "I'm—"

"Shut your bitch ass up!" Jamal hit him with the

gun. He grabbed his backpack and tossed a bundle of money on the floor. "For your trouble, gentlemen. I don't want his body to ever be found."

One of the posing officers picked up the cash and smiled. "Done," he replied.

Chapter Twenty-five

Joe was forced to leave work directly after returning from his lunch. He'd been feeling weak and lightheaded. He thought he could make it through the day and into the evening, but his sweaty palms, mild fever, and the feeling of faintness made him reconsider. The suddenness of his illness had him alarmed.

Paula and Angelo convinced him to leave his car at their office on South 35th Street. They insisted on taking him home in the south suburbs. Their generosity was not uncommon. Police officers look out for police officers, and Joe had worked with Paula and Angelo for years.

He got in the back seat of their unmarked Buick and lay down. His skin tingled, and he started to feel unusually warm. He took his suit jacket off and unbuttoned his shirt.

"You okay, man?" Angelo asked.

"Yeah, I guess." Joe scratched his head. "If I continue to feel like this, I won't be in tomorrow either."

"So where is your little drug-addicted friend?" Paula asked.

"Her name is Reese. And why are you so concerned about her? You want her out of the picture, remember?"

"Nah, I was wrong. She's good for the game." Paula chuckled, and Angelo joined in.

"Okay, that's it, Joe. I don't want to see any more of your fuckin' body. Keep your T-shirt on."

But Joe didn't see the humor. He was too worried. It wasn't like him to be sick. *What the hell?*

Angelo turned around in the passenger's seat. "Damn, man, you're sweating up a storm."

"Maybe you should take me to a hospital instead."

"We can't do that."

Without explanation, Paula suddenly pulled over to the side of the expressway and gave Angelo a nod. In one swift movement, Angelo leaned over the back seat and splashed rubbing alcohol in Joe's eyes, direct from the bottle. The speed of the action and the burning sensation caught Joe off guard, long enough for Angelo to climb into the back seat and dislodge Joe's gun from its holster.

"What the fuck?"

Angelo slammed Joe up against the door.

"Don't give us a hard time, Joe, or we'll shoot you with your own damn gun." Paula watched him in the rearview mirror.

The burning sensation lessened, but Joe continued to keep his hands over his face. "I don't understand," he said, trying to squint through his fingers.

"There's nothing for you to understand," Paula said. "You take your damn job too seriously. That's your damn problem."

"Following the law and honoring my job is being too damn serious? Excuse me for being a law-abiding citizen. I thought—"

"Shut the fuck up!" Paula screamed.

"Angelo, I'm surprised to find you mixed up with her crazy ass."

"Yo, you talkin' a lot of shit for someone in your position," Angelo said.

"What've I got to lose? I'm a dead man, anyway. I always knew that I would die in the line of duty, but never in my wildest imagination did I believe that I would be taken out by my fellow officers. When did this start?"

"We don't want to do this," Angelo said, "but you're putting us in a hole. We have no choice."

"What did I do? I didn't do anything."

"We know you spoke to Internal Affairs," Paula said.

"You're wrong. I didn't talk to Internal Affairs. I didn't talk to no one. They approached Sarge, and he told me."

"Yeah, whatever. But you are not on our side. And this shit is getting out of hand."

Paula scrolled through Joe's cell phone, looking for Reese's number. "It's here. I counted on you to have your drug-addicted bitch on speed dial." She laughed, and exited the car to dial Reese's cell phone.

"Hello," Reese said.

"Reese, this is Carrie, Joe's partner, Chicago PD. Look, we know that you have been working with Joe, trying to assist us to get to Jamal, but there's big shit on the streets now, and you could be in great danger. We have to pick you up now. Right now. Tell us where you're at."

Alarmed, Reese asked, "Where's Joe?"

"Look, Joe's making a bust, okay. Another officer and I are in the neighborhood. We don't have much time. He wants me to pick you up. Where are you?" Paula asked again, the tension in her voice escalating.

"I'm on 71st and Aberdeen. I was—"

"Stay there. Stay right there. It's for your safety. We're coming there now. A blue unmarked Buick. I will have my flashers on, so you will know it's us, okay." Paula hoped she sounded convincing.

"Yeah, sure."

Paula got in the car and looked in the back seat at Joe leaning against the window, perspiring heavily.

Angelo had Joe's hands handcuffed behind him. "Did you talk to her?" he asked.

"Yeah, we're going to get the hoochie now. She's in front of Walgreens on 71st."

"Leave her out of this," Joe pleaded. "Just do what you're going to do, but she has nothing to do with this."

"That's where you're wrong," Paula explained. "She fits too perfectly in the scheme of things, and her drug problem . . . well . . . let's just say that an addict just can't be trusted. Their behavior is so . . ." She paused, looking for the right word.

Angelo joined in. "Unpredictable."

"Right—unpredictable." Paula snapped her fingers.

"You must be smoking that shit, too, if you really think you'll get away with this," Joe said.

"We're already getting away with it," Paula boasted. "By the time they find your body, we'll be thousands of miles away from here, in another country, sipping island drinks, spending our millions on bling-bling."

"Yeah, whatever. I didn't know killing has become your sport of choice."

"Money, Joe, money is my sport and obsession."

Before they approached the block that Reese stood waiting on, Paula pulled into an abandoned garage.

"What up? Why the detour?" Angelo asked.

"We got to put Joe in the trunk, and you're going to have to lie down in the back seat."

"Isn't she expecting to see Joe?" Angelo asked.

"No, Angelo, she's expecting to see me, not Joe, and certainly not you. Besides, we can't drive and keep them both under control."

"But Joe is sick like a muthafucka. His hands are bound. He won't be a problem."

"Angelo, just do as I say and put these handcuffs around his ankles," Paula said, wondering if she overrated Angelo's balls for this kind of job. "We'll know for sure he won't be a problem, at least until we get to his house. She, however . . . we will *make* her ass cooperate."

Paula pulled out her gun, tempted to point it at Angelo to ensure he did as she instructed.

Angelo put the extra pair of handcuffs around

Joe's ankles and pulled him from the back seat of the car. Paula popped open the trunk and helped him to stuff Joe in the trunk, his body too weak to fight back.

"There." Paula wiped her hands clean on the front of her jeans. "Let's go and get Missy Dumb Ass."

"I can't wait until this shit's over. I didn't know we'd have to—"

"I know, I know, but we don't have a fuckin' choice. Stay focused. Within the week this shit will be over."

"I hope so." Angelo edged his hulking frame low onto the cramped floor of the sedan, out of view.

The sedan inched out of the garage into an alleyway and drove slowly until hitting the main residential street. Paula drove northbound on Vincennes and immediately spotted Reese on the other side of the street. The traffic light turned red, but Paula activated her sirens and drove through the intersection, pulling up alongside the curb where Reese stood. Then rolling the passenger window halfway, Paula motioned for her to get in.

"She's coming to the car. Stay down," Paula whispered. The dark tint on the back windows made it impossible to see on the inside.

Paula unlocked the door for Reese to get in the front seat. As soon as Reese got in the car, Paula immediately locked the doors and drove off.

"Where did you say Joe was?" Reese asked.

Paula answered by pointing a gun in her face.

"Don't worry, you'll see him again, Ms. Clark," Paula told her.

Angelo rose up from the back seat, and drew another gun to the back of Reese's head.

Reese gasped, "What?" She reached for the door handle to exit the automobile.

"Bitch!" Paula screamed. "It's locked. But try anything else and we'll shoot your damn head off. Let's handcuff this bitch now." Paula pulled over to the side of the street to retrieve another set of handcuffs from her glove compartment and handed them to Angelo.

"Hands behind your back," he ordered.

As he handcuffed her, Paula tied her feet together.

Reese was too frightened to fight back.

"Please don't kill me . . . please. What do you want from me?"

"Let's stuff her mouth too. Stop her whining," Paula said. "Look, we're not going to kill you . . . not if you cooperate."

"Anything," Reese said. "Anything."

"Good." Paula then slapped a piece of duct tape across her mouth and pushed her into the back seat. "That's what I like to hear."

Paula and Angelo pulled into Joe's driveway, simultaneously breathing a sigh of relief. They exchanged looks, glad they had made it to this point with minimal confusion.

"Let's get this over with." Angelo retrieved keys he had taken from Joe before putting him in the trunk, and exited the car. "I'll unlock his door."

"This is Joe's house," Paula told Reese as they waited for Angelo to return. "I appreciate your cooperation, and like I said before, we're not going to kill you." Her voice remained soft, reassuring.

When Angelo flicked on a light in Joe's house, signaling that he was in, Paula emerged from the car with the gun drawn, pointed at Reese. She walked over to the passenger side of the automobile and grabbed Reese by her collar, forcing her to a standing position. She pulled her out of the car and slammed the door.

Reese was unable to walk because her feet were bound.

"Angelo," Paula screamed, "come get this girl and carry her ass in the house."

As Angelo carried Reese into the house, Paula opened up the trunk to see how Joe was doing. He was lying on his side, vomit running down his mouth. "Damn, Joe," Paula said, "you're really sick." As she strained to pull Joe to a sitting position, she caused him to hit his head.

Joe screamed out in pain.

"Oooops, sorry," Paula said, and she meant it. She struggled to pull his legs out of the trunk, but Joe resisted, weakly thrashing.

"Angelo," she called.

"What would you do without me?" He easily slung Joe over his shoulders.

"What would you do without *me*?" She followed Angelo into the house.

Angelo dropped Joe on his couch in the living room next to Reese, who was now bound down to a chair. She looked at Joe in horror. He was sweating profusely, and his eyes looked glazed over and expressionless. She knew he would be incapable of helping her.

"Told ya you'd see him," Paula said.

"Let her go," Joe said feebly. "She has nothing to do with this."

"We are going to let her go," Paula said. "But you're wrong. She has everything to do with this. I told you she fit perfectly in our plans."

"Let's cut the conversation, and get this shit moving," Angelo said impatiently.

"Yeah, you're right. Where is Joe's gun?"

Angelo placed it on the coffee table and watched as Paula removed thin rubber gloves from her back pocket, put them on, and proceed to wipe the gun clean with the end of her shirt.

"Remove her ties," Paula ordered. "And make her stand." She smiled at Reese as she extended the gun out for her to take. When Reese didn't respond, Paula took the frightened girl's right hand and wrapped her fingers around the butt.

"Now place your index finger into the trigger hole. That's a good girl," Paula said when Reese complied. "How does it feel to hold a gun? Now I want to give you some target practice. If you want to live, you'll have to shoot Joe."

"I can't do that. Please, don't make me do that."

Angelo checked the time on his watch. "We ain't got much time. Either you kill him, or we will kill you."

"Angelo, did you remember to bring the potato?"

"Be right back." Angelo ran back to the car.

"You're not going to get away with this," Joe uttered.

"Still a soldier, huh, Joe," Paula said. "You won't be around to know if we do or don't though." She turned her attention to Reese and took the gun.

When Angelo returned with the potato, she placed it on the nose of the gun to act as a silencer. "Don't want to wake the neighbors," she said smugly. "Now, Reese, get out of your clothes. I want to see your ass butt naked."

Angelo watched hypnotically as Reese removed every shred of clothing, thinking he'd like to have a piece of that ass.

"Angelo, you're salivating at the mouth. Do you want to fuck her? Uncuff the bitch!"

Angelo's eyes danced, and he licked his lips in anticipation.

"I was just joking. Besides, you said we have to get out of here, remember?" Paula pointed the gun in Joe's direction.

His weak eyes stared upward at Paula as her finger tensed to pull the trigger. "You won't."

"I will." Paula laughed. She fired the gun three times at Joe, causing Reese to scream. "And I did."

Reese watched Joe slump to the ground.

"Now, Reese, I advise you to wait ten minutes before leaving this house, and you better think twice about calling the cops. With your fingerprints on the gun, it will be very hard."

Angelo grabbed Paula by the arm, pulling her towards the door.

"Wait! Get her clothing, get a pillowcase out of the closet. Use your head, Angelo. Let's do this right."

After the two officers exited the door, Paula returned with an additional instruction for Reese. "And please don't call the paramedics either.

He'll be dead by the time they get here, and you'll be the one they look at. Believe me, I'll see to that."

Angelo blew the car horn.

"See ya." She saluted, leaving Reese standing naked in the living room near Joe's dying body.

Chapter Twenty-six

Reese watched through the sheer curtains as Angelo and Paula drove away. She remained fixed to the floor, shaking uncontrollably, unable to move. She looked at Joe, who lay inches from her feet. He was changing color, the blood seeping out of him onto the floor. His breaths were shallow and faint. He would be dead in seconds, she thought.

She knelt down to feel for a heartbeat. Nothing. "Oh my God! Oh my God!" She put on her panties left behind in the confusion. She grabbed a T-shirt and trousers from Joe's closet and quickly dressed herself. She saw one of Joe's baseball caps on the bed and put it on.

"He's dead. I know it. But maybe he isn't. Maybe I should call the paramedics," she mumbled to herself. "Maybe they can—Shit!" She grabbed her head, unable to make a decision. She grabbed the phone and dialed 911.

"Hello, hello. Emergency, may I help you?" the operator said.

"I need help. Someone's been shot. I think he's dead."

"Okay, Miss. What is your name and address, so I can dispatch an ambulance?"

Reese dropped the phone on the hardwood floor and ran out of the door, leaving it wide open.

"Hello, hello," the operator said over and over.

Reese walked down the sidewalk in Joe's clothing, straining to appear casual, like nothing unusual had happened. But as soon as she turned the corner onto the next block, she ran with vigor, as though a pit bull were chasing her. She waved her hands frantically when she saw a bus approaching.

The bus driver stopped in front of Reese. "A beautiful girl like you should not be on nobody's bus."

"How much is bus fare?" Reese asked, realizing she had no money on her.

He motioned with his head and closed the door. "For you, beautiful, go on."

Reese ignored the curious stares of the passengers on the bus. She purposely sat at the back of the bus and wrapped herself in the jacket she took from Joe's house. She pulled her baseball cap down over her eyes, buried her face in her hands, and cried.

Reese had no idea where she was going or what to do. The image of Joe's bloody body lying in his living room made her nauseated. she thought she might vomit right there on the bus. She knew the paramedics would locate Joe's house without her giving them the information. They could track the house through caller ID. Perhaps he'd be found alive. But logic told her that he wasn't.

What am I going to do? I have no one to help me. She thought about her short list of friends and acquaintances. "This shit was not supposed to turn out like this." She thought about Jamal's brother's death, her sister lingering in a coma, and now Joe. Reese felt like getting off the bus and walking in front of a Mack truck. Ending her life appeared an easier solution than trying to figure out her next move.

Reese got off the bus at 47th Street. She thought about calling Crystal, but immediately dismissed the idea. Reese found herself walking towards Lake Park Avenue. *Maybe I should just leave Chicago. Hell, nothing is working out here. I can't help my sister; she might die and—Jamal!*

She was supposed to meet him at 8:00. Stopping a passer-by, she asked for the time. It was 7:45. She had fifteen minutes to hook up with him at Sam's Spot. She'd never make it. She dialed his number, surprised that he answered so quickly.

"Yeah?"

"Jamal, it's Reese. I'm gonna be late."

"For what?" Then remembering, he said into the phone, "Shit. I forgot. Somethin' else came up. I ain't gonna be there. We'll have to hook up later. I'll call ya when I know what's goin' down around here."

Reese was clearly disappointed when she hung up. She didn't even have Jamal now. She continued walking aimlessly.

By coincidence, she came upon David's apartment building. She stood outside for over thirty minutes, pacing back and forth, weighing her options. *I would have to tell him everything, but he's a cop. Maybe he can help me. Shit, I don't know which doorbell is his.* As Reese stood staring at the apartment numbers, someone exited the building, allowing her the opportunity to scoot in.

She hesitated at the elevator and pushed 7 for the seventh floor. She got off the elevator and walked towards the end of the hall to David's apartment. She knocked softly at first, putting her ear to the door, straining to hear sound from inside. When no one answered, she rapped again. *He's not at home.*

As she turned to walk away, David opened the door.

"David?"

"Rene, what are you doing here?"

"I-I-" Reese looked down the hallway. She didn't know what to say. "Look, this was a mistake. I—"

"Come in, come in." Seeing her distress, he gently took her arm and brought her into the apartment. "Can I get you something to drink?"

"Whatever you got is cool," she said, following him into the kitchen.

David offered her a glass of orange juice. "Okay, Rene, what happened?"

She gulped it down then studied him. *Here goes.* "Look, I guess I can start by telling you that my name is not Rene, okay. My name is Reese, Reese Clark." She paced up and down the kitchen, stopping only to refill her glass with water from the tap. "Please don't ask me no questions until I finish, okay. I know that you said you were a cop. Anyway, I came here because I have no one else to turn to. I mean, my sister is in the hospital, and I just don't have no one else." She stopped and began to cry huge, uncontrolled, choking sobs.

"Come on." David kindly guided her to the sofa. "Okay, what's going on? You're scaring the hell out of me."

"I'm scared shitless," she said. "I was kidnapped by some cops, and they took me to Joe's house. They killed him, and they got my fingerprints on his gun."

"Cops kidnapped you and killed Joe, and they goin' to pin you for the crime? I was right then— You do know Joe. But it doesn't add up, Reese. What's the real deal? You sound like some damn addict."

"Look, I grew up right here in Chicago."

"What's that got to do with anything? I don't give a fuck if you grew up in Santa Monica, California."

"Just listen, all right, before you judge me. I didn't have a childhood. I mean, my momma, if that's what you want to call her, the woman who gave birth to me and my sister, was not a momma at all. She was more interested in her drugs and men than her own daughters. Anyway, I took care of me and my sister. I fed, clothed, and protected us both.

"As I got older, that shit got hard, so I needed some taking care of myself. I was out there doing whatever with whomever. Anyway, I got mixed up with that fool, Jamal, a small-time hustler when I first met him, but now he runs the whole operation on the south side of Chicago. I thought he loved me. And when you're in love, you do things, stupid-ass things, that you don't want to do, that you think will keep him lovin' you.

"I loved Jamal, and I was fucked up on drugs real bad. I was out there whorin'. Anyway, I shouldn't be telling you this. I mean, I need to get out of here before they find Joe's body and arrest me for murder." Reese jumped up. "I have to, I have to."

David grabbed Reese by her shoulders. "You don't need to go anywhere. I might be able to help you, but I need to know everything."

"Do you know anyone in the Chicago Police Department?"

"A few guys," he said.

"Can you contact them and help me?"

"I need to know first what's going on, before I call or do anything. That makes sense, don't it?"

"I guess. Anyway, Jamal has killed many people."

David held his breath.

"Five years ago Jamal and a friend named Tyrell—I knew Tyrell, anyway. Jamal wanted me to set up a meeting. I thought he wanted to scare Tyrell because Tyrell was coming up in the game. Tyrell was a flirt, so I—" Reese stopped to scratch her arm. "Can I have some more orange juice?"

It took David great effort to keep the disgust he felt for her off his face, but he had to indulge her, had to keep the flow of her story going. He got up to get her more juice.

"Continue," he said, his voice more demanding than he wanted it to be.

"Anyway, I got Tyrell to take me home, and we-we messed around. The whole plan was to get Tyrell to back off Jamal's territory. At least, that's what I thought. I left the door open for Jamal to enter and beat Tyrell up, you know, scare him to back off, but that fool came into the apartment and shot Tyrell right there. He shot him dead and threatened to kill me and my sister if I told. He made me leave Chicago. I pleaded with him not to send me away. I promised not to tell anyone. But I think he saw something in me. See, the light went out in me, and at that moment I hated him. He saw that, so rather than have me killed, he sent me to Detroit and started fucking with my sister. I later found out that she was out on the streets whorin' and druggin'. I wanted to kill that bastard; I still do. I want to pay that bitch back for what he did to me and my sister, but nothing has turned out right. I came back thinking that I could set him up. Joe was going to—" Reese became emotional again and began crying.

"I don't know what to do. It's like, whenever I try to do the right thing, I fuck it up. On top of all this, my sister's brutally raped. She may never recover. Even if she comes out of the coma, she'll never be the same."

Stunned, David shook his head. "So you were helping Joe to bring Jamal down?"

"Yeah, but I was not—I don't know. Joe was not pleased with my cooperation. He wanted me to wear a wire. Lord, what am I going to do?"

"I sensed that you and Joe knew each other, but more than that, I thought he looked at me funny when he saw us at Evergreen Plaza." David snapped his finger.

"I don't know what—"

"Shhhh." David took Reese in his arms. "I'm going to help you."

For a brief moment Reese felt safe in David's arms, but then the overwhelming weight of her situation came into focus again, and she crumbled once again.

Chapter Twenty-seven

Jamal attempted to call several of his boys to get an update on what was going on in the streets, but he kept getting voicemails. He ditched his SUV in Detroit and purchased something far less conspicuous, a maroon '93 Cougar. He drove around 55th and Halsted, looking for anyone he knew. *Ole Manny . . . that fool can tell me something.*

Jamal made a U-turn on 63rd and Halsted and traveled northbound towards the Ole Manny Liquor Store. He parked his car on the opposite side of the street and walked across the busy intersection. As he entered Ole Manny Liquor Store, he thought about Reese and the pictures of her with his father. "I got to remember to call that nasty bitch," he mumbled to himself.

When Jamal walked in Ole Manny's, Ole Manny was leaning over the counter, dropping a handful of candy bars into a young girl's backpack. His hands brushed up against her shirt, stopping at her flat breast for a quick second.

Jamal shook his head in disgust. "Dirty old man," he said out loud.

The young girl, barely 10 or 11, looked at Jamal embarrassed and hurried out the store. Ole Manny grinned at her until she disappeared out of sight.

Jamal looked around the store and was glad to see it deserted.

"I thought you was gone," Ole Manny said. "At least that was the word out on the streets."

Jamal approached the counter. "What else you hear?"

"Depends on how much you got." He wiped off his countertop.

"I ought to kill you, old fuck." Jamal removed his gun from underneath his shirt and grabbed Ole Manny by his jacket.

"That's your problem—you's too fuckin' trigger-happy, instead of using your damn brain."

"Fuck you!" Jamal released Ole Manny and threw a bundle of twenty-dollar bills on the countertop.

Ole Manny grabbed the money and kissed it. "I don't know much, but—"

Ole Manny stopped talking when a customer walked through the door. He walked from behind the counter towards the shopper. "Sir, I'm sorry, but I have an emergency, and I have to close. Sorry." He escorted the customer back outside and turned his sign over from OPEN to CLOSED.

"Like I said, I don't know much, but the po' is pickin' up gang bangers. Jimmy came through late yesterday. Your boy Darren is dead, but you probably know that. That's all I know."

"Which ain't shit!"

Jamal didn't admit that no one had called him about Darren. He felt more and more isolated. "Darren, beautiful baby."

"What a heart!"

"Fuck you, old man."

Jamal walked out the door. He knew where he could find Jimmy and maybe get some more answers to what the hell was going on. He drove to an abandoned building located a couple blocks from Ole Manny's Liquor Store.

Jimmy, a wild but loyal member of the Hustlers, was usually called upon to do the dirty jobs. He had no problem pulling the trigger on anyone, didn't matter the age, sex, or race. Jimmy didn't give a fuck. He didn't care if he lived or died, and Jamal liked that.

Jamal entered the abandoned building through a concealed entrance—a side window. He heard whispers of conversations on the upper floors. He took out his gun and moved quietly up the stairs, careful not to trip over layers of garbage and broken glass. He tucked his nose inside his shirt so as not to breathe in the foul odor assaulting him. He stepped over a drugged-out old man and woman on the floor.

A young lady walked out of one of the empty apartments, and Jamal drew his gun in her direction.

"Baby," she said, startled. She raised her hands in the air. "You need to be careful with that thing."

"Bitch, is Jimmy around?"

The young lady turned and looked back in the apartment. "Maybe. You want Jimmy? Maybe I can help you instead." She walked up on Jamal and caressed his chest.

He slapped her hands away. "There's not a damn thing you can do for me but suck my dick—and I ain't paying."

The young lady rolled her eyes at Jamal and shook her head. "Jimmy, somebody wants to see you," she shouted. She walked past Jamal towards the lower floors.

Jamal bumped right into Jimmy, who was exiting the apartment as Jamal entered. Both drew their guns at each other.

"Fool! Man, I'm sorry, Jamal. Man, I—" Jimmy lowered his gun.

"No problem, dawg. You have to stay sharp." He gave Jimmy the gang handshake and put his gun back inside his trousers. "Jimmy, what the hell's goin' on? I tried calling folks, and nothing. Nobody's returning my calls. It's like everyone is out of Dodge."

"When you left town for a couple of days, shit went crazy. It was almost like you planned the shit. Cops been on our asses like flies. Can't shake 'em, dude. The shit been straight crazy. They runnin' up on everyone, man, from the Hustlers to the Cobras, and the nickel runners too. Man, the jails are swollen with us. They had me caught up, but they didn't have shit, so they let me go. They tried to get me to rat, but you know I ain't like that. I would die before I snitch."

"Bet. What about the money on the streets?"

"Ain't shit happenin', J. The last couple of days

ain't shit moved without the cops running interference. It's as if they know something. I made a contact outside the city. It's goin' down tonight. I'm glad you're back. How did you know to look for me?"

"I got eyes, Jimmy, you know that. You're my man. Tell me about this contact."

"Anyway, since shit ain't been movin', my pockets hurtin', J. I didn't mean to step on your toes, but I'm meeting these cats at Oakwood Cemetery to purchase some bricks of cocaine, approximately a quarter mil worth of shit, man." Jimmy grinned.

"You got the money?" Jamal asked.

"Hell muthafuckin' nah. These Mexican hoods . . . I was simply going to roll on their ass and take their shit and make me a quarter million dollars—I mean, for the organization."

"Mmmm, just like that? That's the muthafuckin' plan?"

"Yep, that's it, simple and sweet. But now since you're back—"

"Nah, nah, let's stick to the script. You set this shit up. I'm likin' what I'm hearin'. I'm in the background. This yo' show. Hell, you're my dawg and partner. I'll follow your orders."

"I didn't mean to step on your toes."

"Quit fuckin' apologizin'. You doin' what any nigga would do, takin' care of business."

Jimmy smiled.

"Mmm-hmm, mmm-hmm," David repeated.

Reese looked at him from the couch where she sat balled up in the corner, chewing her fingernails nervously. She glanced down at some photos tucked under a Bible on the coffee table. She reached over to get them, anything to keep her mind off her troubles.

The first was a picture of David and what looked like his mother. She noted the strong resemblance. The next was of David and his mother again. The third photo caused her to jump up from the sofa and give a short scream. She saw David, his mother, and Tyrell posing for the camera at what appeared to be a dinner engagement.

"Oh my God," she shouted.

David looked at Reese then at the photo she'd dropped to the carpet.

"Sarge, I'll call you right back," David said firmly. "Gimme ten minutes."

Horrified, Reese looked at David.

"I can explain," he said calmly.

Reese was shaking too hard to hear. "Oh my God, oh my God, Tyrell is your brother? Oh my dear God."

"Yes. Come here." David grabbed her two arms to settle her then carefully led her to the couch.

Reese, too agitated to sit, jetted back to her feet. "Oh my God, you're a cop. You could be mixed up with this. Oh my God, you's gonna kill me."

"Look, you need to calm down. I'm not going to kill you, and I'm not mixed up with this situation, I promise you."

"How do I know that? How do I know that you won't kill me?"

"If I wanted to kill you, I could have a long time ago. Think about it, Reese."

* * *

"J, I got something to show you." Jimmy led Jamal to another empty apartment building. "You know, Darren came by here asking stupid-ass questions and looking for you. Word on the street said he met with the Cobras."

"You killed him, huh?"

"Had to—one bullet to that muthafucka's head. Had to be done. Had to watch your back."

"Man, a nigga appreciates that." Jamal peeped into the bedroom, where Darren's lifeless body lay.

"Look, man, we got to jet if we goin' to meet those muthafuckas on time." Jimmy checked his watch. "Man, I wish we had someone else with us, like a broad or somebody, to check out the scene and shit."

Jamal dialed Reese's number. "Say no more." He smirked. "I know just the bitch for the job."

Chapter Twenty-eight

"Look, Reese," David said reassuringly, "if I trust anybody, it's my boss, okay. And this plan will work, but you have to stay cool."

"But what if he notices?" Reese buttoned up her shirt. "Jamal is not dumb, you know."

"How in the world is Jamal going to know that the threads on the shirt are wires, and those buttons are actually mic speakers, unless you tell him?"

"Maybe he can figure it out because the shirt is so damn ugly. Kinda seventyish, don't ya think?"

"Not on you. Look, Dan pulled some strings for me to help you, and if you pull this off, you will be cleared of everything, and dirty-ass Jamal will be behind bars for life."

"And that will satisfy you? I thought you wanted him dead."

"I thought you wanted him dead too."

"I do, but life in jail will have to do. I just want to get on with my life and help my sister."

When Jamal called and told Reese to meet him later that night, David had to scramble to put everything in place. Usually set-ups took time, everything being accounted for, down to the last detail. This, however, was happening too fast. On top of that, Jamal's meeting place didn't feel right.

"Now tell me again where you're going to meet him."

"We were supposed to meet at Sam's Spot, but he changed it to the Oakwood Cemetery . . . something about a gang meeting. I don't know, he was vague about it. Now you're sure your people know about this?"

The look on David's face confirmed what she was thinking.

"Don't you think that's odd, meeting at a cemetery?" she asked. "You sure they can hear me through this thing? They will be out there?"

"Yes, to both questions, Reese." David tried to sound more reassuring than he felt. He kissed her lightly on the forehead. "I want you to know that nothing will happen to you. It's a promise. I'll be there watching with the others. I will be looking out for you."

"Really? You sure about that? I thought you wanted me dead too."

David exhaled. "Reese, this is not the time to discuss this, okay, but I will tell you, I believe Jamal used you to set up Tyrell, okay. We have a common enemy, remember that. Stay focused, and don't blow your cover. Your life depends on it."

"Thanks," Reese said weakly as she walked out David's door. "That's what I needed to hear."

As Reese stood outside the apartment building, looking to hail a taxi, her cell phone vibrated in her pocket. *Jamal*.

"Hello."

"Reese, don't go to the cemetery. Meet me at Ole Manny Liquor Store instead."

Chapter Twenty-nine

The nurse hummed softly as she did her usual scan over Tracey's chart. Nothing had changed from the day before. She then exchanged IV bags and checked her vitals, noting that her temperature remained high. Not significantly, but enough to keep her on antibiotics. The nurse touched Tracey's cheek. It felt warm to the touch, so she took a cool, wet cloth and patted Tracey's face and arms. That was when she heard the first sound, almost a moan.

She turned down the piped music that the doctor ordered on a continual run into Tracey's room for sensory stimulation, customary for coma patients, and she heard it again—a soft, low groan, almost painful-sounding. The nurse studied Tracey carefully for any other sign that she might be breaking through her coma—fluttering eyelids, mouth movement, anything.

It came, but not on her face. It was her arm. Tracey was attempting to move her left arm.

"Oh my goodness," the nurse said excitedly. "Dr. Mathews, it's Tracey."

"What is it?"

"She's moaning, and I saw her trying to move her left arm. That's a good sign, isn't it?"

"Maybe so." Dr. Mathews placed his stethoscope on Tracey's chest. "Or it might be a neurological reflex. That's classic for these cases."

"No, Dr. Mathews, she's moaning like she's in pain. She's coming out of that coma. I know it."

Dr. Mathews smiled to himself. In his experience, nurses' premonitions proved true, more often than not. He studied the screen on the intensive care monitor, looking for any change in her bodily activities. Finding nothing of consequence, he turned to the nurse. "Have you talked to her sister?"

"No, but I would love to give her the good news."

"Please don't tell her any more than what really is going on. We don't want to get her hopes up, and if we're wrong—"

"I will simply tell her that her sister is being more responsive."

"Very good."

The nurse sang softly to herself after the doctor left the room. "And she's coming out of that coma."

Chapter Thirty

Jamal picked Reese up in front of Ole Manny Liquor Store. Reese, looking for his SUV, was surprised to find him behind the wheel of a rusty Buick Cougar.

"Get in," he demanded as he pulled up along the curb. Before Reese could close the door, Jamal hit the gas pedal, almost causing her to fall out of the car.

"Damn," Reese said as she managed to close the passenger door. "What's the rush?"

"You better be glad that I didn't throw your nasty ass out."

"What ever happened to meeting at the cemetery?"

"Plans change."

"Oh," Reese mumbled under her breath as she fidgeted with her fingers. "Did you ever find out who killed Jun-Jun?"

Jamal slowed down and looked at Reese from the

corner of his eyes. Then he reached over and opened the glove compartment and threw a picture on her lap. "You one nasty bitch," he said. "Carmichael was my pops."

Reese looked down at the photo. It trembled in her hands.

"You ain't got shit to say?"

"I-I-I didn't know that Carmichael was—he never mentioned, and . . ."

"Get your damn story straight. You didn't know, or your nasty ass didn't care?"

She didn't respond.

"Anyway, did you know that fool flipped both ways?"

Reese continued to remain quiet.

"And he's dead."

"What?" Reese gasped. "How?"

"And you really care?" Jamal snickered. "That fool was lit when he got in a car accident. Never came out of that damn coma. Anyway, my aunt Charlene stated that dude contracted some nasty shit. I believe it was gonorrhea or herpes or something like that. Oh well, his punk ass is dead." He looked at Reese disapprovingly. "Your ass might have given him that shit, whatever he got. I'm glad that I didn't touch your nasty snatch. I would kill you if—"

"I didn't give him nothing."

"Shut the fuck up!"

Jamal turned his car onto a side street and stopped without pulling over. "Look, I don't give a fuck, okay. But a friend needs your help and I'm dropping you off right here."

"A friend? Who is that? What help he want from me? Jamal, don't do this. I don't know him."

"All you need to know is that his name is Jimmy. I don't know what help he needs, but whatever it is, I advise you to cooperate."

"But—"

"But nothing. Get out and wait for him here."

He picked up his cell phone and dialed Jimmy's number. "Yeah, dawg, she's here. You pullin' up? Good . . . yeah . . . see ya."

In his haste to drive off, Jamal didn't see the black '88 Dodge follow him as he drove randomly through the Chicago streets.

"Sarge, our men are in place."

Exhausted, Sergeant Smith flopped back in his chair. He'd been in his office for over twenty-four hours, trying to set up a sting operation to catch Angelo and Paula. He blew his stack when he learned that a separate federal sting operation was taking place on his turf and that he was not informed of their set-up. On top of that, they expected his cooperation.

"I want my boys out there too," he shouted into the speakerphone. "This is supposed to be a collaboration. I don't trust your men."

"That's not an option, Sergeant. We can't jeopardize the safety of our men for—"

"But your secrecy might have cost the life of one of my men, a damn good detective."

"Hey, hold on. Knowing about tonight wouldn't'ta stopped one of your own from taking out your detective. I appreciate that this is coming down fast. Hell, we didn't learn about it until tonight, but one case don't have nothin' to do with the other. We had to work fast."

"Maybe," Sergeant Smith said, "maybe not."

Chapter Thirty-one

Jimmy pulled up as Jamal sped off. He called out Reese's name before she had an opportunity to change her mind.

Reluctantly, she got into his car.

He removed a big duffle bag from the passenger seat and tossed it in the back seat to make room for her.

"So you Reese?"

Reese shook her head yes.

"Look, I don't know if Jamal told you or not, but what I need is simple, and I will pay you for your troubles. I simply want you to confirm whether or not a car is in a designated spot, and I want you to drop off that bag in the back seat. You do that, and I will get you two grand for your time of less than . . . mmm . . . ten minutes."

Reese looked over her shoulders. "What's in the bag?"

"Now, that's none of your damn business. Drop

the bag, call me on this cell phone, and your part is over. I will meet you later with Jamal and give you your money, honey."

Reese scratched her head. "Identify a car, drop the bag off, and that's it?"

"Elementary shit. I think you can handle that, right?"

"Yeah," Reese replied. "When we do this?"

"The show begins in thirty minutes . . . at the cemetery. You aren't afraid of dead people, are you?"

"Should I be?"

Jimmy removed his gun from underneath his seat. "It's the alive muthafuckas that you should worry about."

Jimmy drove down Cottage Grove towards Oakwood Cemetery. He cared little that Reese was in the car when he spoke brashly into his cell phone. "Jamal is a punk. I set this damn deal up, and I'm going to keep the muthafuckin' money. I might give him a piece of the bone, just because—Hell nah, he ain't runnin' shit!"

Reese felt her phone continually pulsate from incoming calls, but she was afraid to answer it. "I wish I could see Tracey," she mumbled to herself.

"Huh?"

"Just talkin' to myself."

"I hope you ain't no crazy ass. I don't need that."

He pulled up to the entrance of the cemetery and studied the terrain, looking for anything suspicious. "Look," he said seriously, "that bag in the back seat is what needs to be delivered in that cemetery." He pointed. "Two Mexican-looking dudes will be in a black 4-door Chevy Impala. One dude has a ponytail, and you can't miss 'im. Anyway, you're going to bring me back a bag just like the one in the back seat, okay?"

"What if they don't get me the bag?" Reese asked.

"Why wouldn't they?"

"I don't know. Do they know I'm comin'? Where you gonna be?"

"Look, don't worry about that. I will be around. That's all you need to know. Just drop the bag off, grab the other bag, and come back to the car."

They both looked up to see a small procession of cars speed into the cemetery, mostly teenagers in pickups and old-model cars, hooting and hollering out the windows, waving beer cans in the air, shooting up gravel as they raced in.

"What the fuck—? Who comes out late at night to visit the dead?"

"Kids," Reese told him, getting ready to grab the bag and exit the car.

Jimmy motioned for her to stop. "Wait . . . you can't go in there with those drunk bastards."

She smiled, hoping that the plan would be called off. "What now?"

"We wait," he replied, irritated.

They lingered quietly, listening to the voices in the distance, the horns blaring, motors gunning.

When the sounds stopped, Jimmy said, "They're gonna stay and party with the dead, those cock bastards."

If she were ever asked to describe the eyes of a killer, Reese would think of Jimmy. She'd say they flickered, moving over objects in a fast, jerky motion, but when he zeroed in on something, they stood unblinkingly still. His eyes would jump from area to area, looking for anything wrong. Then he'd turn his eyes on her, without provocation, and burrow into her with a long, unflinching stare that scared her to the core. That's how she felt as they waited for nearly thirty minutes before the line of cemetery night crawlers left in the same blaze they had entered.

"I need to see if my contact is still in there, but I don't want them to see me. Maybe I should just send you in. You can walk in the shadows." His fingers tapped nervously on the dashboard.

They watched an elderly, hunched-back man walk out of the entrance of the cemetery and begin to pass their car, headed towards a lone car on the street, a Ford Focus. They imagined him to be security.

Jimmy jumped out of his car and pointed his gun at the man's head. He shouted for Reese to grab the bag and get in the car, but she froze.

He pointed the gun at her head and shouted, "If you don't bring your ass on, I will shoot your ass from here." Jimmy moved his gun back and forth from the elderly man to Reese.

Reese broke out of her daze and grabbed the duffle bag from the back seat and rushed towards the car.

"Look, nobody's gonna get hurt," Jimmy explained to the frightened man. "I simply want you to drive us into the cemetery. I'm looking for a black Impala. It shouldn't take no more than five minutes. Now get in the driver's seat and turn on the engine." He motioned with his head for Reese to get in the back. "Don't you try any dumb shit either. Nobody'll get hurt if you follow the script."

What neither Reese nor Jimmy knew was that Jamal spied the whole interchange from the tinted windows of his borrowed Ford Taurus. His plan was to simply jack Jimmy for the drugs and money, or whatever he had.

The elderly man's foot sputtered nervously on the gas pedal as he drove deeper into the dark, deserted cemetery. Jimmy didn't see a black 4-door Impala. Nor did Reese see any signs of the police.

"Those muthafuckas, they gotta be here. They suppose to be here over an hour ago." His eyes flitted nervously over the cemetery grounds, and his agitation grew.

Finally he shouted, "Stop the car. That must be them over there." He pointed to an automobile with its emergency flashers on. "I want you to drive a couple more feet ahead. Then, Reese, you take it from there. Exchange the bags and run back to this car." Then he added, "There's only one way out of this muthafucka, so don't get any funny ideas. If you don't come back, he's dead. And give me your damn cell phone."

Reese got out of the car, leaving the elderly man in the car, and Jimmy's hand securely fixed on the trigger.

Jimmy lowered the gun and pointed it directly at the old man's side. Reese heard the fear in the elderly man's breathing as she softly closed the door. She was too afraid to look into his eyes.

* * *

"Why in the hell did they close the gates?" David asked from inside the surveillance van.

"We got them," one of the DEA officers announced. "Let them broker the deal, and we'll move in and nab everyone."

"How do you know that you've got everyone? We haven't heard Jamal's voice. How do we know he's with them?" David asked.

"Trust me, he's with them," the agent said. "I've been doing this type of operation for a long time. He's around."

Jamal watched suspiciously as the gates of the cemetery automatically closed. He got out of his car and walked in the shadows along the metal fence surrounding the cemetery.

He attempted to call Jimmy, but he got his voicemail. "Cocky fool."

As he walked back in the same direction from which he came, Jamal saw a woman and her child standing near the hood of his car. "Damn!" He walked over to his car, gun cocked and ready to shoot. When he got close, he instantly recognized his son, Jabaree.

"Daddy, Daddy," Jabaree screamed out excitedly, straining to run to Jamal. But he was unable to move. The woman's right arm held him securely to her.

When she raised her left hand in a cool fashion, exposing her gun, Jamal lowered his.

"Who are you?" he asked. "Do I know you? What are you doing with my son?"

She stroked the top of Jabaree's head. "Mmmm . . . he's a nice-looking young man, don'tcha think?

How old is he, three or four? Sons are precious, very precious. I had a son a little older than yours."

Jamal squinted his eyes, trying to recognize the young lady. "Okay, whaddya want? How much do you want?"

"There's no money in the world you can give me. I want my son to come back from the dead. He's buried in there, ya know." She cocked her head at the cemetery.

Realizing this woman meant business, Jamal tried to hide the fear in his voice. "Look, lady, that's my son. I'm sorry to hear about your son, but I don't know who you are."

"That's sad, truly sad. I don't believe you came to his funeral either. Nah, I didn't see you because, if I did, they would have been reciting your eulogy."

Jamal's mind raced with a million ideas about how he could get out of this situation alive with his son. He had no doubt that if he raised his gun to shoot her, she would shoot Jabaree. She had the gun resting comfortably across his chest.

She could see Jamal's mind search for an escape hatch. "I advise you to throw your gun away," she demanded.

When Jamal hesitated, she shouted, "I'm not playin'!"

Jamal tossed his gun on the grass. "Now what? Who in the hell are you?"

"I don't understand. You must be stupid or something, still trying to go for bad, even in your situation."

"Look, I don't know who the fuck you are. You got my son, that's all I know. I don't know what the hell you want."

"Is your car door unlocked?"

"Yeah. Why?"

"Open it."

He moved slowly to the car, hoping to gain time to figure out his next move.

"Jabaree, I want you to sit in the car while me and your daddy talk some more."

Jabaree looked to his daddy for permission.

"Jabaree, go sit in the car, okay," Jamal said with quiet authority. He watched Jabaree do as instructed then he slammed the door shut.

"You have a sweet son. Obedient. I like that."

"You told me that. Now are you going to tell me who the fuck you are?"

"You think you in control, don't you?" Angela pointed the gun at Jamal's left knee and pulled the trigger.

Jamal screamed as the bullet penetrated the bone, bringing him to the ground.

"Since you keep askin' who the fuck I am, I will tell you. Does the name *Anthony Paxton* ring a bell?"

Horrified, Jamal grabbed his bleeding knee and looked into Angela's eyes.

"I'm Anthony's mother, or I was." Angela's tears dripped on her upper lip. "But you took care of that. I'm no longer a mother. I'm nothing. My world died when you killed my—"

"I didn't kill him." Jamal held his knee to stop the blood from gushing out. The pain was excruciating.

"Nah, you just told some punk to kill my son. Darren told me that you gave the orders, so you killed him too."

"Look, your son killed a young girl."

"He was trying to be like you. My son looked up to you."

Jamal tried to stand on his left leg. "I never meant—"

Angela raised the gun again and shot him in the other leg.

"Damn!" he said, his voice hoarse and full of pain. "Why don't you just kill me? Why in the hell are you shooting me like this in front of my son?"

Angela looked in the car at the young face pressed up against the window. "Your son is young. He will get over this and forget about you. He'll be better off. How do you feel?"

"Fuck you, bitch! Just go ahead and shoot me."

"Nah, that'd be too good for you. I want ya to bleed to death." Angela raised her gun and shot Jamal a third time in the stomach.

Angelo sat on his car horn, trying to get Paula to hurry up. *She shoulda had her bags packed and ready to go.*

Their drug busts did not bring them the funds they anticipated, and now they were trying to leave the city with less than $350,000, splitting it 50/50. Paula had suggested that they take Amtrak out of Chicago, until they reached the West Coast, and then drive on to Mexico.

Angelo thought about everything that transpired. He knew the consequences were not worth his $175,000—the murders, the set-ups, everything. Regret moved through his heart, slowly turning to anger, mostly at Paula for having seduced him into this. *One more death won't matter; in fact, I will be doing CPD a big favor. Hell, I'm a wanted man.*

He watched Paula emerge from the apartment, a bag tossed across her shoulders.

Yeah, one more murder won't matter much.

As Paula opened the door to the station wagon, Angelo fired his gun one time, shooting her directly in her chest. She gave Angelo a bewildered look before falling back onto the concrete.

Sorry, Paula, but I had to do it. You understand $175,000 is simply not worth all the trouble we went through; $350,000 is not much better, but I believe you were getting ready to do the same thing.

Angelo drove off, feeling vindicated. Ya do whatcha gotta do. He wasn't prepared, though, for the bullet Paula managed to fire off before she died, hitting him squarely in the back of the head.

Reese jumped with each gunshot she heard pop off in the distance. She prayed Jimmy hadn't shot the old man held hostage in his car. She continued walking to the dark-colored car parked across a gravel path only thirty feet from her. Reese hated that she had to step over tombstones. The thought of dead bodies reaching out of the ground to grab her ankles occurred to her.

As she got closer, she noticed an individual standing outside the car. She could see the shadow of a gun in his hand. She iced up in fear, unable to move another step forward. Reese looked behind, aware that Jimmy was out of her sight and unable to see her in the blanket of darkness.

Another gunshot echoed in the distance, startling her into movement. She dropped the bag on the grass and ran randomly in the blackness. Lost in the line-up of tombstones, she tumbled into them as she fled, uncertain how to escape. She kept running until she saw a light ahead of her, at the entrance, she hoped. She talked in the air, praying her voice carried through the wires on her shirt. "David, I'm lost. I'm in the cemetery running to a light. I think it's the front entrance. Please help me. I'm so scared. I heard shots. Please come get me, please." Her words left her mouth as short blasts of air, both fear and her running literally taking her breath away.

Jimmy could no longer see Reese and concluded she should have reached the car by now without any problems. He was about to call her on the cell phone but remembered that it sat next to him on the front seat.

Jimmy looked over at the elderly man, who sat trembling. "I said I'm not going to kill you." He tried to sound reassuring, but he wasn't known for having a soft spot, for saying the right encouraging words. "Don't have no heart attack in this muthafucka, or I will shoot your old ass." He laughed. That was the best he could do.

Reese's phone rang, and Jimmy picked it up. "Hello."

"Reese, is that you?" David asked.

"Who this?"

"Who is this, and where's Reese?"

"Who the fuck wants to know?"

David looked at his cell phone and hung up. He

sat in the surveillance van and, through binoculars, watched a small body in the distance move around aimlessly through the cemetery. He'd heard her pleas for help and wanted to tell her he could see her. He wanted to tell her to keep running. He knew there were other unmarked vehicles on the inside. Why they hadn't moved in to assist her confused him. *Whose side are they on anyway?*

"Get the gates open," David ordered the agent. "I'm goin' in. I promised I'd watch her back, and I'll keep that promise."

The federal agent jumped up in David's face. "You're not going nowhere."

"Yeah? Try and stop me. Far as I know, those gunshots we heard were meant for her. Now open those fuckin' gates. She's on her way."

"That's why we didn't tell your sergeant about our operation—too many chiefs and cowboys, too many egos. You're about to blow our cover."

"Shut the fuck up! I don't think you guys know what you're doing . . . 'cept talkin' shit."

With that, David bolted from the surveillance van.

Chapter Thirty-two

Angela stared down at Jamal and watched a thin line of red trickle down each side of his mouth.

"I know that you ain't goin' to leave me like this," Jamal managed to say, his voice choking.

She liked that his words only increased the flow of blood, forming a pool inside his mouth, causing him to gag. When he attempted to lift his torso, she kicked him swiftly on the head. Then she thought of her son and spat in his face.

The wail of pain he screamed out was music to her ears. She smiled as she looked on his face twisted with pain, his teeth colored with blood, his body shaking convulsively. *Yeah, you gonna die right here*, she thought to herself.

"Could ya hurry and die? I want you to take your last breath while I'm here to watch, you son of a bitch." She glanced over her shoulder when she heard footsteps on the gravel. She saw the shadow of a body running in her direction. She had just enough time to kneel over Jamal and put out a cigarette on top of his forehead.

He could only manage a silent, open-mouthed scream.

Angela hoped it was only a matter of minutes before he was dead. She looked back at the car, at Jarabee's face pinned to the window, calling out, "Daddy, Daddy."

She had no intention of harming the boy, at least not physically. She knew he'd be mentally damaged, but what choice did she have? What she didn't know, though, was that little Jabaree's face would forever haunt her dreams at night and her thoughts in the day. She'd see his open mouth screaming out to his daddy.

Time to get out of here.

Angela looked up to see a female on the other side of the metal gate.

"Miss, please help me, please. I need your help to get out of here. Please help me." Reese, now running across a small pathway, pleaded with Angela, and for a moment it seemed like she would wait. "Please," Reese screamed, "they're going to kill me. I need your—"

Then a booming voice called out from the darkness, "I'm coming, Reese, I'm coming."

Reese turned in the direction of David's voice and saw him at the entry, beckoning her forward. She ran with all the speed her strength would allow.

They hugged through the bars.

"Oh, David, David," she cried. "I gotta get out of here. He's parked over there with a gun."

"He who?" David examined the gate's security lock. The agents had refused to raise the automatic gate.

"Jimmy. He's a friend of Jamal's, and he's holding an old man hostage," she rambled, knowing she made little sense to him.

She panicked when she heard the roar of a car engine starting up. She put one of her legs through the iron bars and strained to push her whole body through. "He's coming, he's coming. Oh God, I got to get out of here."

Observing that the width of the bars was too narrow for Reese to squeeze through, David told her she'd have to climb up. It was her only option.

"Look, I can lift you on my shoulders, and you can pull yourself up towards that bar and climb over and jump. I'll catch you."

"I can't. I just can't, David. It's too high."

"Look, the car is coming. You don't have much time. Get up there, climb over, and I'll catch you. Damn! The worst that can happen is you'll fall and scrape yourself. That shit's better than getting shot."

David lowered himself and maneuvered his shoulder partially through the bars, allowing Reese to grab hold and position one foot on top of his shoulders while she pulled herself up. Reese was able to grab the top bar, approximately eight feet above the ground, and climb over.

David had his arms outstretched, waiting for her to jump. She wavered as she looked down at him, but as she heard the car speeding close in, she jumped with such force that they both fell to the ground. "I'm sorry," she whispered.

"Shhhh." He quickly got to his feet, pulling Reese up with him, and dragged her into the thicket behind the brick wall.

"We got to get out of here."

They watched the car speed up to the gate, only to find it closed. The vehicle then made a U-turn and backtracked into the cemetery. They could see its tail lights drive from sight.

"Shhh, you're safe." David cradled her in his arms. "You're safe. Calm down."

Both Reese and David were startled by a high-pitched scream.

"What was that? Where's that woman trying to start her car?" Reese pointed towards the abandoned vehicle.

"I don't know. Somebody's still over there." David stopped talking as he heard the sounds of a car door slamming. "Shhhh." He put his index finger to his lips. He guided Reese by the arm, down the brick wall towards the sound. "We need to tell them"—David pointed to the police surveillance truck—"that you're out and they need to call for back-up."

David reached in his pants pocket to retrieve his cell phone. "Yeah, she's safe. She's with me. They're still in there, holding an old man hostage. You need to get back-up. . . . Yeah, I got you. . . . Someone down the way is hurt, on the outside. I'll check it out then we're on our way."

David pulled out his gun and cocked it, moving cautiously along the gate. He indicated to Reese to follow closely behind.

The two nearly tripped over a body. Reese and David were stunned to see Jamal lying helpless on the cold concrete, his body shaking and drenched in blood.

"Well, well, well . . ." Reese moved his arm with her foot. "What goes around comes around."

David bent down to assess Jamal's condition. "He needs a paramedic."

"Hell, nah." Reese slapped the cell phone out of David's hand, and it shattered as it hit the ground. "Let the muthafucka die right here. He doesn't deserve no help, not after the shit he done to you and me. He killed your brother, remember?"

"I don't need you to remind me. Let's go."

"No, I want to see him die. I want to see him take his last breath."

"Let death take care of him. We need to get you back to the police surveillance truck, and try to clear your name."

"I bet that lady shot his ass. Probably a jilted hoochie. Too bad she left. I would have liked to thank her."

"You sure it was a woman?"

"Yeah, she was a sister. She tried to get away in that car, but it wouldn't start. I guess she made do on foot."

David looked at the abandoned car and wrote down the license plate number. That was when they looked up into the terrified face of a little boy staring out the window of the old Cougar.

Chapter Thirty-three

An interview with a dead gang banger . . .

*D*arren Paxton, known as Dirty D, was found mur-dered in an abandoned building in the West Engle-wood Area. The résumé of his life is typical. He grew up in the poorest section of Chicago in a single-parent house-hold. His father was not involved in his upbringing, and he dropped out of high school in his freshman year. The streets were an easy magnet for him; it taught him the game of survival in all the wrong ways. His closest friends were gang bangers, so naturally he walked a sim-ilar path.

He was a troubled youth, and grew into a more trou-bled adult. He was known in the juvenile justice system, as well as the adult criminal court system. He fathered children, but never participated in their care. Police have alleged that he was a cold-blooded killer. (Informants say that's how he acquired the name Dirty D.) He was a poster child for all the negative statistics that plague

African American males. But there was one statistic he surpassed—he lived beyond the tender age of 21. He died at 24.

Darren Paxton was a menace to his community, and I'm sure many are not mourning his death. The story of his life is a portrait of wasted possibilities, and his death would go unnoticed, mourned by the few that truly knew him.

Who was Darren Paxton? He was everything that I previously stated, but that was only a small part of who he was. We would never know the person that he was capable of being.

According to his mother, he loved to tell jokes and keep his family members laughing until their sides ached. He was a brother, loved and despised at times because of the life he chose, but nevertheless, a sister is grieving her brother's untimely death. He was an uncle to Anthony Paxton.

An avid reader of African American literature, and a gifted street poet—His sister shared with me his journal that he kept hidden from the world—Darren Paxton's poetry reflects the harshness of the life he lived, a dosage of social consciousness sprinkled between the lines.

I had an opportunity to meet Darren before his untimely death. I do not profess to know him; much of what I learned came from those who knew him best. But in the short amount of time we spoke, I was able to peep into his world and see a man bitterly torn about the decisions he'd made.

How many Darren Paxtons or Denise Paxtons are living next door to us? Young boys and girls struggling with the perils of life—drug abuse, poverty, single-parent households, chaotic neighborhoods.

Many of you will send me e-mails stating that you live in similar conditions without succumbing to the evils of the streets. I applaud your strength and determination. Maybe you had a mother, father, or family member that kept their hands around your neck, threatening you along the way, and wavering wasn't an option. Maybe your faith was rock-solid. Yes, there are many whose stories do not end up like Darren Paxton's, yet there are many more whose stories are never written, their history reduced to the rap sheets and police reports that authored their lives.

I wrote this column today to show how easy it is to sit in the comfort of our homes and judge the "troubled youths" terrorizing our streets. Some of them need to be incarcerated and punished for their crimes. And some of them need an understanding heart to help them pave a better way. Darren Paxton was a menace to some, hated by others, but mostly misunderstood.

I'm closing this commentary with two of his poems, "How Do I Continue to Have Hope?" and "Where Is Cabrini Green?" I hope that after you read these poems you will have a deeper perception of the Darren/Denise Paxtons that may live next door to you.

How Do I continue to Have Hope?

How do I continue to have hope
When all I see from my window are pieces of shattered
dreams
Scattered on the urban concrete
Tainted with my brother's blood
Yet, my brother that died last night
And identified this morning with no name
His death was celebrated over a cup of coffee
As the number of drug-addicted was minus one

But do believe that another brother just took his first hit
And is about to take that trip that my other brother
could not come back from

And my sister,
She's tripping too
And my momma don't care
Daddy nowhere to be found
And we're all choking from despair
How do I continue to have hope?

Playgrounds are dirt-filled lots
And schools have become war zones
Learning to survive is the lesson plan
And I no longer feel safe at home
How do I continue to have hope?

I want to get out
But I don't know how
The path used by those before me
Do not exist now
How do I continue to have hope?

Where Is Cabrini Green?

Where is the dirt that existed underneath my feet?
As I walked over broke dreams and mean-ass streets
Where is the piss that hiss behind closed doors
Trash scattered on concrete floors
And hope and love do not breathe anymore
Where is the pipe that contained the smoke
Of Daddy's absence
And Momma's coke

As she screams over dying dreams
And the realization that the white man's scheme
Existed long before I was conceived
But my brothers and sisters were fools to believe
That equality could be achieved in a prison of walls
Stacked twenty stories high
Maybe a view of Lake Michigan
Made them believe that they can coincide
With them?
Where is Cabrini Green?
But he's not the only one lost
My brother, Robert Taylor, also paid the ultimate cost
Now my brothers and sisters wear this look of despair
Wondering why the white man don't care
And that the day has arrived for the termination
of welfare
We choose to complain
Instead of understanding their game
This relocation of my people is no joke
And yet, we refuse to go to the polls and vote
Now
They're looking for my brothers, Cabrini and Robert
But I'm also crying for my sister Ida
For she too has died
Along with Henry Horner and Alba right by their side
And Rockwell
Was yesterday's hell
And Stateway
Is no longer in the way
For this is a new day
Called gentrification
A plan for a paler nation
Now my brothers and sisters,
I hear their screams and cries

As they're held prisoners on the far south side
Riverdale, Dolton, Markham, and Hazel Crest are
the new nests
For my people
But with suburban living
We still are not considered equal
Where is Cabrini?
Where are our ghetto homes?
Forcing us out of Chicago to these southern and western
places to roam
Where is Cabrini, and will he ever be found
Or has he become a memory in this racist-ass town?

I hope everyone who reads this looks past the exterior of the Darren Paxtons in our community and helps them unlock their talents. This was the first time he was published. Rest in peace, Darren. You are missed.

       —*Lisa Stillman*, Chicago Chronicle

Chapter Thirty-four

"Clear, a second time." The doctor placed the simulators' plates on top of the man's chest.

"No response," the nurse shouted back.

"Clear, a third time," the doctor said.

The emergency room medical personnel were working vigorously to bring the gunshot victim on the gurney back from the brink of death.

The doctor, unwilling to give up, tried several more times to stimulate the victim's dead heart.

A nurse softly grabbed his arm, a quiet gesture that told him what he already knew—the victim was beyond his assistance.

"He's dead," the nurse said. "We did all we could."

Dr. Blackman stood back and sighed and gave a quick nod, a gesture of thanks to his staff. He then silently removed his mask and gloves and walked out of the operating room, leaving the rest of the medical staff to tend to the body.

Five gunshot victims and four deaths under his watch during the last twelve hours. Dr. Blackman wanted desperately to save this last victim. He *needed* to save the last victim.

"Doctor?"

The doctor looked up at a man waiting with pad and pencil in hand. "Journalist?"

"No. I'm detective Matlock with the CPD." The detective handed Dr. Blackman a business card with the Chicago Police Department logo and showed his badge.

"What's the status on Mr. Angelo Santiago?"

"Well, officer, your Detective Santiago is dead. He didn't make it. I'm sorry."

"Don't be." The detective wrote on his note pad. "Dude was dirty. Your staff shouldn't have wasted their time trying to revive him."

"Well, at our hospital our policy is saving lives, not judging them."

"What was the exact cause of death, doctor?"

"Gunshot wound to the head. If you have any other—"

"Don't worry, we'll subpoena your records." Detective Matlock nodded his head and turned away without so much as a thank you or good-bye.

Two Chicago police officers walked up on Reese and flashed their badges, announcing that she was under arrest.

"Hold up, wait a minute," Reese yelled. She looked to David for an explanation.

He looked as stunned and surprised as her.

"What's going on? What the hell are you doing?" He stepped between Reese and the officers, blocking them from using their handcuffs.

"Stay out of this," Sergeant Smith said, "or you will get arrested too, for jeopardizing an investigation."

"What the fuck are you talking about? This was all pre-arranged. She helped you nail Jamal, and this is how you show your gratitude?"

"This has nothing to do with Jamal," Sergeant Smith said. "Your little druggie friend here set up Joe to be—"

"Wait a minute. You know damn well she had nothing to do with that."

"What you *think* you know and what may be the truth should be left up to the investigators. You know better than that, David. Besides, she left the scene of the crime," Sergeant Smith said, weariness in his voice. "We only have her word for it. Now step aside."

David watched helplessly as the officer lowered Reese's head and guided her to the back seat of the squad car. He knew the sergeant was right.

Reese's bewildered face pressed against the cold window. She mouthed the words, "Help me."

As the vehicle pulled away, Reese saw a little boy standing with a female officer. She recognized him as the child in the old Cougar. *Poor kid.* She had no way of knowing this was her nephew. She had never seen him.

"What about the kid?" The female cop gently held Jabaree's trembling hand. "What we going to do about the kid?"

Sergeant Smith scratched his head. "I don't want to take him down to the station with us, but damn, we gotta find out who he is. DAMN!"

"Sergeant," the female cop whispered, "you're frightening the kid. Look, I'll make a hotline call to DCFS, let them know it's an emergency, all right. Tell 'em we'll meet them at McDonald's."

She rubbed Jabaree softly on top of his head. "Hungry?"

Jabaree nodded his head yes.

The sergeant appeared relieved. "Thanks, Officer Jones, I owe you."

"No prob, and don't worry." Officer Jones led Jabaree to her squad car.

Chapter Thirty-five

"Mommy, please don't hurt us. We just was getting something to eat." Tracey ducked to avoid her mother's fist. "No," she screamed in terror and ran over to the corner of the kitchen where her big sister, Reese, was huddled.

As Tracey darted over to the other side of the room, Reese grabbed the broomstick perched behind the refrigerator and started to swing it wildly.

Tracey stopped and looked at her sister, then back at her mother.

Reese motioned for Tracey to get behind her.

"Bitch, I know you ain't gonna hit me with that broom," Veronica said.

Reese looked at the broom, confused.

"I'm gonna beat your ass too. I told ya not to go in that icebox, hungry asses."

"We just wanted something to eat." Tracey hoped that her mother would leave her alone.

"I don't give a damn, little wench. Y'all some

hardheaded muthafuckas. I'm gonna teach you a lesson that you gonna remember forever."

Reese positioned the broom over her shoulders again, preparing to swing if necessary. "Leave us alone!" Through her fear, Reese found her voice, and spoke commandingly. "Leave us alone!"

Her words only encouraged her mother to step forward, laughing all the while.

Reese pulled the broom back and, in one quick step, swung with all the force her small body could muster.

"My, my, Missy." Veronica touched her cheek, where the bristles lightly brushed her face.

It took nothing for her to yank it out of Reese's hands. "Bitch, I don't know what devil possessed you, but I'm gonna find him and beat him out of you."

Reese dashed past her, running into the living room.

"Yeah, your ass better run . . . cuz I'm comin' after you." Veronica walked slowly back into the living room, where Tracey, now pinned between the sofa and wall, sat crunched up tight into a ball, making herself as small as possible, her head buried in her arms.

"Tracey, go get me that belt out of my room."

The small child looked up to see the large figure hovering over her. When she didn't move, her mother bent down over her and grabbed her cheeks with her fingers and squeezed, bringing Tracey's face up to meet hers. "I-said-get-me-that-damn-belt," she said, emphasizing each word.

Tracey could only nod in compliance.

When her mother finally let go, Tracey ran to her

bedroom in search of the belt. She saw it and quickly hid it under the bed. She opened dresser drawers, then slammed them shut, calling to her mother, "I'm looking. I can't find it. I know it's here someplace."

Given enough time, she knew her mother would forget about her. The drink always worked that way on her mother.

Just when Tracey began to feel things were returning to normal, she heard her sister's piercing wail followed by a loud thump against the wall.

"Reese, Reese," Tracey shouted.

The nurse, startled by Tracey's words, ran out into the hallway to alert the doctors. "Come quick. It's Tracey. She's coming out of it."

Chapter Thirty-six

"We got the security firm on line two. They can deactivate the security lock on the gate from their office. He said he will take less than a minute. Our men are ready to go in when they receive the signal."

Jimmy saw the flashing red lights outside the gates of the cemetery. "Where's that trick at? And why are the gates locked?" He stood outside the door of the Ford Focus. He watched as headlights slowly moved towards him.

Jimmy jumped back in the car and pointed his gun at the elderly man. "Get out!"

The elderly man, weak from fear, attempted to pull himself out of the car.

When he took too long, Jimmy yelled, "I said get out." He then reached in and yanked the man out by his coat.

"You said you wouldn't hurt me," the elderly man said, his voice small, his breathing labored.

"I don't give a fuck what I said." Jimmy pulled the elderly man in front of him for cover.

A dark-colored car slowly pulled up to face the two men, illuminating the area with bright lights.

"What the fuck you want?" Jimmy squinted his eyes against the strong light.

A bullhorn sounded, "This is Chicago Police. You're surrounded inside the cemetery, and we have men waiting outside the gate. Put your weapon down, and let the man go. No one will get hurt. Drop your weapon and let the man go."

Jimmy pulled the elderly man closer to him, to use his body as a human shield. The police stepped from the vehicle, their guns drawn.

"I don't give a fuck about this man, so you better back off." He began a slow move backwards, out of the light, holding the old man securely in front. "Get back!"

"Let him go," the officer announced on the bullhorn. "You're surrounded."

Jimmy continued to move back, away from the car and the lights, forcing the elderly man to follow awkwardly. The uneven terrain caused Jimmy to stumble, but he quickly regained his footing and continued his retreat, only to trip a second time, causing the elderly man to fall, bringing Jimmy down with him.

The gun discharged in the air, and the police returned fire.

Hearing no more shots, they ceased fire and moved closer to Jimmy and the elderly man. They were sickened when they found the two bodies unresponsive, covered with blood.

"They're both dead," one officer said, stating the

obvious. "He shot his gun at us. He fired his weapon first."

"Yeah, he fired first, just remember that."

"I know, I know. I just didn't want . . . I mean, the old man is dead. The Office of Professional Standards is going to investigate this."

"It was self-defense, man, it was self-defense. Always remember that. He sent out the first shot."

Chapter Thirty-seven

Conversation whirled around Reese as she rode to Cook County Jail with other female detainees. She held her head down as she listened to them chatter on about their solicitation charges or drug bust, their attitude so casual, you'd think they were comparing shoe sizes. Not wanting to show weakness, she preferred they not see her eyes swollen from crying, but they couldn't miss her runny nose, which she tried to wipe on her already-soaked shirt sleeve.

"Can you please loosen these handcuffs? My wrists are hurting badly." Reese lifted her hands in the air.

"Ms. Princess is in a little pain," one detainee teased, causing the others to laugh. "You haven't seen pain yet. What ya charged with?"

Reese stared out of the window.

"Stuck-up-ass bitch, I asked yo' ass a question. Don't act like you don't hear me."

"Shut the fuck up, Wanda!" the guard shouted out from the front of the bus. "That goes for everybody else too. Ya goin' to the County Jail, not on the *Jerry Springer Show*. If you don't shut up, I have something that will make ya." He cocked his rifle and lifted it in the air.

"I hope he shove that piece up his ass," Wanda whispered. "Princess, I'm not finish with yo' ass, dissin' me and shit."

"SHUT THE FUCK UP!" the guard said again, this time walking to the center of the bus, staring Wanda down, daring anyone else to whisper a sound.

Only the humming of the engine and the guard's heavy steps could be heard as he walked slowly to the back of the bus.

Reese took a swift look up into Wanda's angry eyes and quickly lowered them when she blew her a taunting kiss.

"Both should be charged with attempted murder," the district attorney said after reviewing the charges against Reese Clark and Angela Paxton. "The media is all over their story. People are lining up and taking sides, so we have to be very careful how we handle these cases. There'll be a lot of sympathy for Ms. Paxton, but not much for Jamal Winters, though. The public is sick of the gangs. The media will be down our backs, a real headache, and with elections coming up—"

"But first degree? Are you sure? After all, Ms. Paxton's son, Anthony Paxton, was murdered less than three months ago. It was her only kid. You want to charge her with attempted murder because she went after her son's killer? Remember, he was only eleven years old," the assistant district attorney argued.

"Yeah, but remember, he was responsible for that little girl being shot. That'll all come out in court, if not before. Then the public says that he got what he deserved. Shit, it gets complicated. Besides, we can't condone vigilante justice. I hope that Winters recovers quickly to have his day in court. I know what I'm doing, Maureen. Don't keep second-guessing me on this. It's wrong to excuse street justice, even when we think it's the right outcome. That's wrong."

"Okay, boss, it's your call. I just want to be sure we review all the options. I mean, Ms. Paxton doesn't have a criminal background like our other girl, Reese Clark. Ms. Paxton is a hard-working, ten-year food service employee at St. Bernard Hospital. She's a loyal churchgoer, and—"

"Her beloved son was a gang banger."

"And? I'm sure she did the best she could with what she had. Children sometimes go bad, despite the love, nourishing, and caring they receive at home."

"Maureen, my decision is final. You keep forgetting the little boy she kidnapped. That's unconscionable. What was she thinking? Angela Paxton will be charged with the attempted murder of Jamal Winters, child endangerment, and kidnapping. Reese Clark will be charged with the first degree murder of Tyrell Porter and attempted murder of investigator Joe Black. I'm requesting they be held without bail." She slammed her pencil on the desk and looked up proudly, confident of her decision.

Chapter Thirty-eight

Sergeant Smith, never known for his patience, slammed the phone down a third time. He'd dialed John Stronger Hospital repeatedly for a status report on Joe, and every time, he was transferred from the Emergency Room to the Intensive Care Unit to Recovery, shuffled from one person to another for over ten minutes. "That's it." He grabbed his coat from the back of his chair.

Just then, David stormed into his office. "Why no bail for Reese?" He banged the office door shut.

Sergeant Smith held his right hand out in front of him, preventing David from coming closer. "Hold up, cowboy. I don't have time to deal with this shit. I'm on my way out."

He sidestepped David to reach the door, but David backed into it first, blocking him.

"Look, I don't have time for your bullshit, all right." Sergeant Smith looked down at his watch. "I'm on my way to John Stronger Hospital to check on Joe's status. We know your precious, innocent friend was involved in him getting shot. And if you weren't a cop . . . I don't know. I should investigate your angle in all of this."

"Look," David said more calmly, "she wasn't involved. I know it. She's been through so much. Her arrest just seems like overkill."

"I can't help you now, and to be honest, she is my last priority. It's in the DA's hands now. My mind is on Joe. He's in surgery, and I can't get no info over the phone. So, please, can we take this matter up at another time?"

"Yeah, we can. I hope Joe pulls through this. We are friends, Joe and I, you know, not close buddies, but colleagues who liked each other, and he—"

"Look, if it's as you say and she had nothing to do with this, then you better hope he pulls through. Who better to tell us what happened? Maybe he can clear her."

"He definitely doesn't deserve—Sorry, I just remembered that I have another friend at John Stronger Hospital, and I was wondering how she's doin'. Can I ride with you?"

"You come into my office, cursing me out, and now you want to ride with me?"

David was about to comment, but Sergeant Smith raised his hand, motioning for him not to utter a word. "Come on."

As the bus pulled into the Cook County Jail, Reese looked up at the tall barbed wire fence and security towers strategically placed around the facility. Reese had been arrested a couple of times and held at district police stations, but never transported to Cook County Jail, a real hellhole.

Her worst confinement was in Detroit, when she was admitted into an inpatient drug center. The first week was hell, because she had to earn the privilege to leave the facility, and then only accompanied by a staff person. However, as time passed, Reese recognized the importance of embracing the opportunity to get her life together.

Now it looked as though she was still paying for her sins, and even some she didn't commit. As the guard yelled for the detainees to stand, Reese wiped her eyes with her sleeve again.

Wanda said, "Don't worry, princess, this ain't shit to cry about. Just wait."

Reese ignored her.

As they lined up in the aisle of the bus, Reese spotted a familiar face far ahead of her in the line, but before she recognize who it was, the guard was pushing her down the aisle to exit the bus.

The detainees were escorted down a long hall, the chains around their hands and ankles rattling rhythmically. Reese remained on high alert as Wanda continued teasing her.

They continued their regimented walk in line until they reached "the gray room," where they changed out of their street attire into bright orange jumpsuits, the DOC logo boldly advertised on the back, compliments of the county.

The guards ushered three female detainees at a time into the gray room. Reese began a mental count and was relieved that her tormentor would be in another threesome. Her prayers went unanswered though, when the guard called another woman out of line, thereby placing her nemesis in her group.

The three female detainees were instructed to line up against a wall and remove all of their clothing. Reese hesitated as the other two started to shed their clothes without embarrassment.

"What cha waiting for?" one of the guards asked. "We said take off all of yo' clothes—NOW!"

Reese jumped and started to undress, kicking off her shoes first. Then she began to slowly unbutton her top.

"You must have some sweet stuff that you don't want to show nobody. Don't worry, sweetie, I'll keep your secret and taste it later."

Reese looked up to see Wanda standing fully naked, thrusting her hips at her. "You must be crazy," Reese told her.

"You haven't seen crazy, bitch."

The guard looked at Reese, the last one to remove all of her clothing. "You, shut the hell up and strip like we said. You talk too damn much."

Finally Reese stood with the other detainees, butt naked against the wall. A chill of shame filled her, leaving her vulnerable and believing this was one of the worst times in her life, even worse than when she was on the streets soliciting and drugging. At least the drugs medicated her pain. There she stood in a room full of hostile strangers, exposed, defenseless, and with absolutely nothing to hide behind.

One of the guards approached her. "What's your name?"

Reese shuddered. She didn't answer, a look of confusion on her face.

She gave Reese a sharp poke on her shoulder. "I said what's your name?"

"Reese," she said softly.

"Step over here, please."

The guard moved to the far side of the room, and Reese followed quietly, listening to the catcalls and whistles from Wanda.

The guard, having heard enough, pointed to Wanda. "You better chill." Turning to Reese, she said, "I need for you to turn around, squat, part your butt cheeks, and cough."

"I don't have anything on me."

"Do as I say. This ain't a tea party. We don't have all day to wait on you. Either you cooperate, or we will force you to cooperate. The choice is yours. Squat, part your butt cheeks, and cough."

"I need a tampon," another female detainee announced. "I feel my menstrual coming down."

"What's going on tonight?" the guard asked. "This is not really happening. We have a prima donna here that don't want to follow rules, and now a bleeding bitch. Look, we got fifty more inmates to process. I'm wasting no more time on you, Reese or whatever your name is. Do as I say, period."

"Can I get a tampon?"

"Hell nah, you just stay still. And you"—The female guard pushed Reese slightly—"get with the program."

Reese looked at the other female detainee and saw small droplets of blood spattering around her feet. Exhaling her last ounce of dignity, she bent over and coughed.

Chapter Thirty-nine

Justice or Politics?

*District Attorney Whitney Paige held a news confer-
ence regarding the arrest of Angela Paxton. She spoke
adamantly about her desire to prosecute Ms. Paxton to
the fullest extent of the law. Ms. Paxton has been charged
with the attempted murder of Jamal Winters, child endangerment, and the kidnapping of Mr. Winters' son
from his foster placement. Ms. Paige acknowledged that
she will recommend that no bail be granted for Ms. Paxton.*

*I wonder if Ms. Paige is sincere in her decision to go
after Ms. Paxton. Ms. Paxton is the mother of Anthony
Paxton, the 11-year-old who died almost 3 months ago to
gang violence. Anthony was also the nephew of the Darren Paxton I wrote about in an earlier article for our
"Gangs in Our Streets" series. Is she seeking justice, or is
she driven by the desire to get re-elected in the upcoming
weeks?*

While I don't agree with Ms. Paxton's actions, Ms. Paige has colored her as a menace to society. She is a woman grieving, driven by vengeance, but by no means is she a danger to our community. Her church has rallied behind her, trying to persuade the parties to at least grant her bail while her case is being processed through the court. Ms. Paige stated that she would block any move to grant her bail. Is she motivated by justice or politics?

—Commentary by Lisa Stillman

Chapter Forty

Sergeant Smith parked his unmarked squad car outside the main entrance of John Stronger Hospital. He leaped out of his car before he could comfortably put it in park, and quickly flashed his badge at the security guard moving towards him, ready to tell him that he was parked illegally.

The security guard acknowledged the badge and allowed the sergeant and David to enter the hospital. David followed on Sergeant Smith's heels, jogging to meet his hurried pace.

Neither man spoke on the ride to the hospital. David looked over to his driver a couple of times, but knew not to engage him in conversation. His deep scowl and intense concentration on the road told David not to aggravate him.

As the sergeant walked through the ER, his badge ready, he grabbed the first nurse exiting the double doors and demanded assistance. "I'm trying to find out what's going on," he told her. "I've tried calling and calling but keep getting the runaround. I need to know the status of one of my men."

The nurse walked over to a computer station. "What's his name?"

"Joe . . . Joe Black. He's an investigator with Chicago Police Department. He was airlifted here from Saint James Hospital."

The nurse input the information and wrote the data on a piece of paper. "He's still in surgery," the nurse told him after pulling Joe's file up on the computer screen. "That would explain why you had problems—"

"Is he okay?"

"I'm sorry, but we won't know until the doctor comes out."

"How about Jamal Winters—what is his status?"

The nurse typed in the name. "He's out of surgery, and in Room 421."

"Do I need a pass? He's under hospital arrest."

"No, not a pass, but you will need to show our medical staff your badge," the tired-looking nurse said, about to get up from the computer.

David told her, "I don't want to bother you, but can you tell me the room number for Tracey Clark?'

The nurse rolled her eyes at David and sat back down at the computer to look up his request. "Tracey Clark is in our Intensive Care Unit on the seventh floor. I take it you're a cop too."

David nodded his head and walked away.

"Cops are so ungrateful. They could at least say thank you."

*   *   *

Reese let out a deep sigh once they finished searching her and allowed her to put on the bright orange jumpsuit.

The guards now turned their attention to the bleeding detainee, becoming really concerned when they saw the small droplets of blood quickly escalate to a large clot. They quickly took her to the medical unit for examination.

Reese was finished with her intake and assigned to Division 11. As she was escorted into the large dormitory, she caught a glimpse of the female on the bus, who she thought looked so familiar. *That was the woman at the cemetery, rushing to get away in the car.* Reese smiled when she put two and two together. *She's the one that shot Jamal.*

Reese decided to approach the woman, who sat alone at a table. "Hi."

Angela looked up at Reese and then back down at her folded hands.

"My name is Reese." Reese extended her hand, but Angela didn't look up.

"I remember you near the cemetery. I was the one calling to you for help," Reese whispered.

Angela didn't respond.

"I simply want to thank you. You took care of Jamal. It was something I was planning on doing."

Angela looked up at Reese. "What do you want?"

"Nothing," Reese replied. "Nothing at all. I didn't mean no harm. If I'm disturbing you—"

"No, no, I'm sorry. My name is Angela." Angela put her hand over Reese's.

"I'm not usually mean, but this place"—Angela looked over shoulders—"is worse than hell. And . . ."

Angela couldn't finish her statement. She put her head down on the table and began a desperate cry.

Compassion swelled in Reese. She knew she didn't have the words to console Angela, so she said nothing.

Finally Angela raised her head. "I don't need to be here. And what I did . . ." Angela paused before screaming, "Anthony!" at the top of her lungs. To everyone's horror, Angela jumped out of her chair onto the top of the table, yelling Anthony's name over and over in a feverish rage.

Reese scooted away to a safe distance and watched the guards intervene, subduing Angela, and immediately transporting her away. Reese heard the words "psychiatric unit."

Again Reese felt alone in the dormitory. She walked over to a far corner and sat on the floor and wrapped her arms around her knees, reminding her of when she was a small girl and she would escape her mother's anger by hiding in the corner of the living room.

A detainee said, "Another crazy-ass bitch."

Reese knew she wasn't referring to Angela.

Chapter Forty-one

"Yes, she has regained a degree of consciousness, but she is reliving a psychological trauma. We believe it's one that occurred in her childhood. She calls everyone either Carolyn or Reese. Our psychiatric team is evaluating her. They have temporarily diagnosed her with severe post-traumatic stress disorder with psychotic features. The bleeding on the brain has diminished, but we aren't certain about the long-term effects. We know that Reese, the name she is mumbling, is a sister, but we're not sure who Carolyn is. She's getting stronger, but it'll be a while before we discharge her. We still don't have much info on her. In the interim, she's ready to be taken out of Intensive Care."

"Is she aware of the fact that she'd been raped?" an intern asked.

"No," Dr. Mathews replied. "She is not oriented to time and place. Psychiatry is not my background, so I will try and explain this the best I can. It's like her mind is stuck and cannot release itself. We are going to monitor her some more.

"Unfortunately, there is no medication known to shorten the duration, or bring her to a higher state of consciousness. We have to take it a day at a time and watch for any changes, even small ones. We'll meet every day for updates." Dr. Mathews placed Tracey's file aside and opened the next one in the stack. "We have a gunshot victim coming to the floor. He's touch-and-go. I see he's currently under police supervision, but I don't think that they have officially arrested him. I don't want a lot of officers on the floor until I have more information. We need to get him stable and transferred to the County medical unit. Any questions?"

No one responded.

"Just so you know beforehand, before reading about this in the paper, the woman arrested for shooting him is Angela Paxton. Apparently this was a vigilante shooting. I won't go into details. You'll hear about it on the news. His name on the record is Jamal Winters."

Nurse Jasmine walked into Tracey's room and was pleasantly surprised to find her sitting up in her bed, sipping her water, watching Court TV. The nurse turned down the volume and walked over to her bed to take her vitals. "How you doin', sweetheart?" she asked, lowering her bedrail.

"Fine, Momma, just fine," Tracey replied in a child-like voice.

Nurse Jasmine smiled and rubbed Tracey gently

on her shoulders. "I'm not your momma, sweetheart. But I'm sure glad you made it through this ordeal. God is blessing you, and He's going to help you through this. I will continue to pray for you. Are you hungry?"

"Yes, yes," she replied with enthusiasm.

Nurse Jasmine laughed at Tracey's sweet innocence, thinking that it was her way of escaping the truth of what brought her into the hospital in the first place. "Okay, good. I will call food service and tell them to bring you a plate right now." She picked up the phone and dialed the extension to food service and ordered Tracey a dinner of roast beef and mashed potatoes. "I hope you like the food. It's pretty good at times," she said, trying to engage Tracey in conversation.

As the nurse wrote notes in Tracey's medical chart attached to her bed, the food service worker entered the room.

"That was fast."

The food service worker smiled and placed the tray down on the table that sat across the room. Nurse Jasmine positioned the over-bed table close to Tracey and brought the tray over. Tracey watched carefully as Jasmine removed the cover off the entrée and took the fork and spoon out of its protective covering.

"Mmmm, this smell good," the kindly nurse said.

Tracey reached for her fork and started to eat her mashed potatoes.

"Good, you eat up, okay. I'll be back shortly to check on you." Nurse Jasmine walked back to the nurse's station. Just then an orderly was transporting Jamal up to the floor on a gurney.

"He's going to Room 5, but it's not quite ready. Give us ten more minutes," Nurse Jasmine said.

"We're not taking him back down. He'll wait right here."

As the orderly turned to leave, a police officer walked through the door.

"You can sit down right there." Nurse Jasmine pointed to a chair near Jamal's gurney. "We're getting his room ready now."

The police officer pulled out his newspaper and started to read the sports section.

Meanwhile, Jamal, conscious and resting on his gurney, and beginning to feel the absence of the pain medication given to him before surgery, began to moan. The nurse approached his side and reassuringly told him to be patient, the room would be ready momentarily and he would get his medication then.

Tracey finished up her mashed potatoes and looked up at the TV screen. Earlier, Nurse Jasmine had turned down the volume, displacing the controller.

Tracey got up to look for it, but, in the process, forgot what she was doing and exited her room shoeless, her gown open in the back, still holding the plastic fork, and potato leftovers running down her mouth onto her shirt.

Nurse Jasmine looked up to see the disoriented Tracey walking down the hall. "Baby, you should be back in bed," she said from the nurse's station.

Tracey continued to walk haphazardly until she reached Jamal's gurney.

"Tracey, Tracey," Jamal said, surprised to see a familiar face.

Tracey stopped and looked at Jamal, then smiled in recognition. "Momma," she said.

Jamal laughed. "What the fuck's wrong with you? I ain't your momma. It's Jamal, stupid ass."

Tracey turned her head from right to left, as if to clear her head. She pointed her finger at him.

The police officer looked up briefly but resumed reading.

"Jamal," Tracey said. "Stupid."

Jamal laughed again, but only until Tracey raised her left hand with the fork and stabbed Jamal directly in the throat.

The police officer looked up, too late to stop her, and rushed Tracey, pushing her up against the wall.

"What's going on?"

"She stabbed this man," the police officer said, dumbfounded by what had just happened.

Nurse Jasmine immediately called the operator with "code gray."

Chapter Forty-two

"My client is entering a plea of not guilty," the lawyer announced on Angela's behalf.

She sat somberly in a blue pinstripe pantsuit with a white blouse. Her eyes remained fastened to the table as her lawyer stood arguing on her behalf.

"I want bail to be granted, Your Honor. My client has experienced enormous distress, and she will be better served in a psychiatric hospital than the county facilities. She is no danger to society. She has an extensive favorable work history, has never been involved in the criminal justice system, and has the unwavering support of the community."

The district attorney argued, "Your Honor, she deliberately and maliciously attempted to murder a young man. She kidnapped his son, Jabaree, from his foster placement and placed him in danger as she engaged in torturing his father. The child watched from the window of the vehicle. I believe that no bail should be granted for her. We should base our decision on the facts, not the cries of the community."

Angela's lawyer exclaimed. "Your Honor—"

The judge banged her gavel. "I know the facts. Ms. Paxton's bail will be set at $500,000."

"Thank you, Your Honor." Angela's lawyer looked at her client and smiled.

"I don't have that kind of money, even at ten percent," Angela whispered.

"Don't worry. Your church has set aside funds for your bail. They have raised up to $100,000 for you thus far, monies to use for your attorney fees, so you don't have to worry."

Angela closed her eyes, clasped her hands together, and said a silent "Thank you" to God.

Chapter Forty-three

Three months later . . .

R eese walked out of the Cook County Jail, surprised that she was being released until her trial date. She was informed that her bail was granted at $100,000, and that an anonymous donor paid the amount needed for her release. She picked up her personal belongings from the central intake processing unit and walked out of the gated entrance to 26th and California.

Reese knew that her counselor from Detroit and Crystal had worked tirelessly from the outside to help with her release. She was ordered to enroll in an extensive drug treatment program.

During her two and a half months of incarceration at Cook County Jail, Reese was visited by David once. She tried to call him when she had phone privileges, but she could never reach him. She had apologized over and over to him, and while he'd said he accepted her words, she knew that his heart could not forgive her. Reese heard the good and bad news about her sister's recovery, and rejoiced over Jamal's death.

Reese wrote extensively during her incarceration. She wrote about her mother, her childhood, and her pain. The writing became therapeutic. She'd begin writing in the morning after chores, and she'd write until the siren sounded to eat. Reese wrote at every available moment, trying not to allow the effects of jail to enter her spirit. She wrote and wrote until her fingers ached.

As she walked outside the jail walls, she saw a blue sedan parked across the street with the shadow of someone in the driver's seat, obviously someone to pick up one of the other inmates being discharged with her. She watched as the others ran to meet their loved ones, knowing, sadly, that there was no one to share in her release. She forgot to ask Crystal or her counselor who would pick her up, or if anyone would pick her up.

She started walking as the others drove off with their families and friends. Only the sedan was left behind. She became nervous that whoever sat in the car might be someone from her past, someone who wanted to do her harm. She looked over her shoulder and saw a man leave the blue sedan. He was holding a bouquet of balloons and walking in her direction.

Reese raised her hand to her open mouth, and tears spontaneously flooded her eyes when she recognized David. She ran into the street, meeting him halfway, causing cars to blare their horns, but she didn't care. "I wasn't expecting to see you here," she said, almost too afraid to be happy.

"I know," David said, "but after everything that happened, and . . . well, I spoke with Crystal and told her I wanted to pick you up. Just me, no one else."

"Really, thank you," she said. "I thought you wrote me off. I haven't been able to get in contact with you, and you only visited me once—"

David put his finger on Reese's lips. "Shhhh. I have a lot of explaining to do, okay. But we have plenty of time to discuss the details. I'm taking you home."

"Home? I don't have a home. I thought I was going to enroll in a drug treatment center."

"Well, you can if you want to, but Crystal and I convinced everyone that you'd been drug-free for a year, with only one relapse . . . all this prior to your incarceration, not because of it. So you'll be allowed to participate in outpatient therapy. Anyway, I rented out a house in Hyde Park, and you can do your rehabilitation there with me. Look, it's your decision, if you're not comfortable—"

"No, I want to," Reese said eagerly.

David smiled and led her to his car. "You need to know that your sister is getting better. I've arranged for you to visit her in the next couple of days."

"How is Joe?"

"He's coming around—imagine that—by the grace of God. He's in a wheelchair, but that hasn't stopped him from rallying in your defense. He described everything that happened that day. Reese, you've been through too much for one little gal. It's time for you to heal."

"I owe you so much . . . so much."

David smiled. "Just get yourself together. I'm here to help."

ABOUT TWELVE

TWELVE was established in August 2005 with the objective of publishing no more than one book per month. We strive to publish the singular book, by authors who have a unique perspective and compelling authority. Works that explain our culture; that illuminate, inspire, provoke, and entertain. We seek to establish communities of conversation surrounding our books. Talented authors deserve attention not only from publishers, but from readers as well. To sell the book is only the beginning of our mission. To build avid audiences of readers who are enriched by these works—that is our ultimate purpose.

For more information about forthcoming TWELVE books, please go to www.twelvebooks.com.